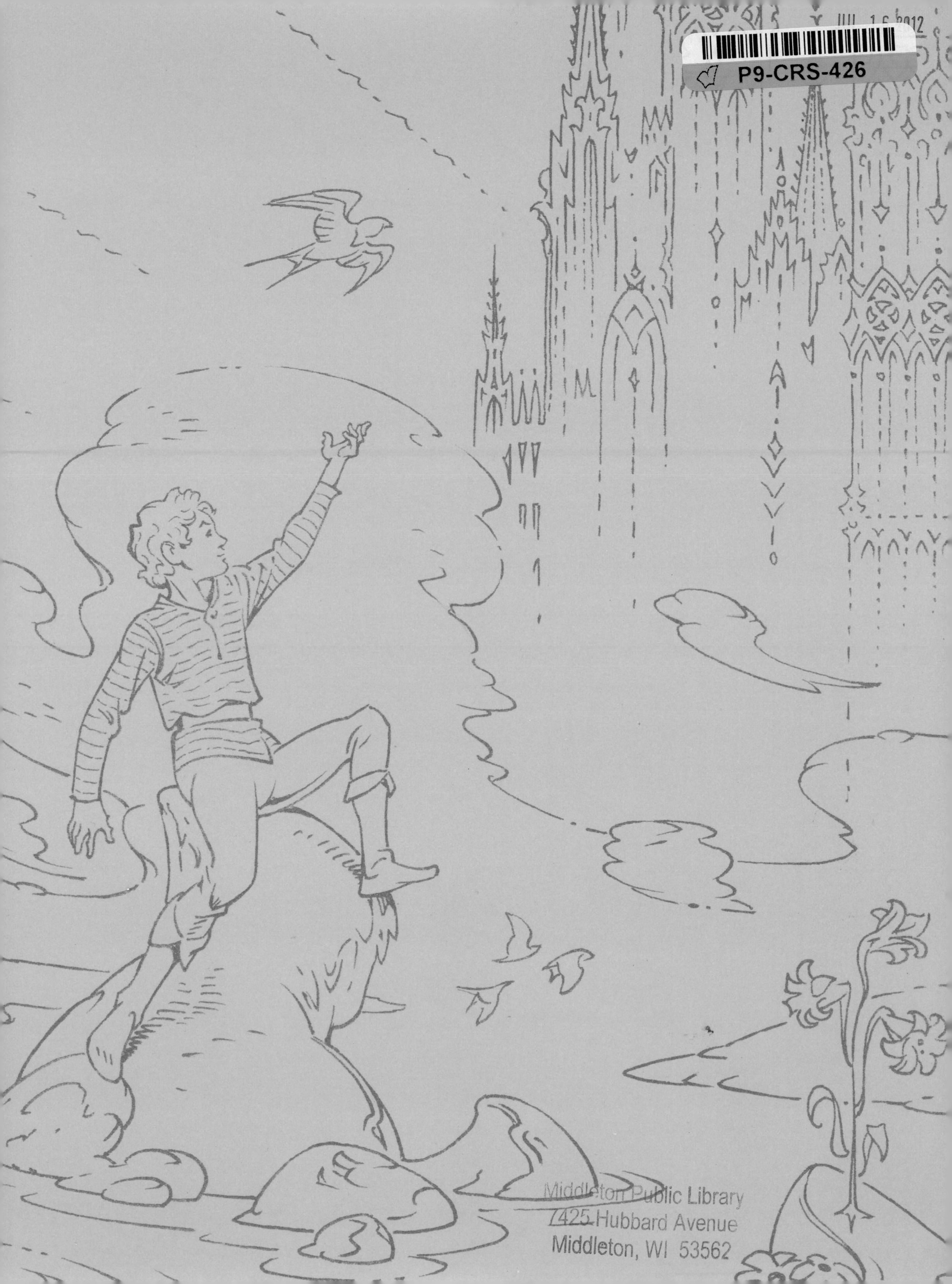

FAIRY TALES OF OSCAR WILDE

ILLUSTRATED ★ BY

P. CRAIG RUSSELL

THE HAPPY PRINCE

NANTIER · BEALL · MINOUSTCHINE
Publishing inc.
new york

Also available by P. Craig Russell:
FAIRY TALES OF OSCAR WILDE
Vol.1: The Selfish Giant and The Star Child, $17.99 hc., $9.99 pb.
Vol.2: The Young King and The Remarkable Rocket, $15.95
Vol.3: The Birthday of the Infanta, $15.95
Vol.4: The Devoted Friend and The Nightingale and The Rose, $16.99 hc., $8.99 pb.
OPERA ADAPTATIONS:
Vol. 1: The Magic Flute
Vol. 2: Parsifal, I Pagliacci
Vol. 3: Pelleas & Melisande, Salome
Each: $24.95 hc., $17.95 pb.
Set of Three paperbacks: $44.99
($4 P&H 1st item, $1 each addt'l)

See previews and more at www.nbmpub.com

Write for our complete catalog of over 200 graphic novels:
NBM
40 Exchange Pl., Suite 1308
New York, NY 10005

ISBN 978-1-56163-626-6, cloth
ISBN 978-1-56163-629-7, signed & numbered

Library of Congress Control Number: 2012932579
Colors by Lovern and Jesse Kindzierski
Printed in China

1st printing, April 2012

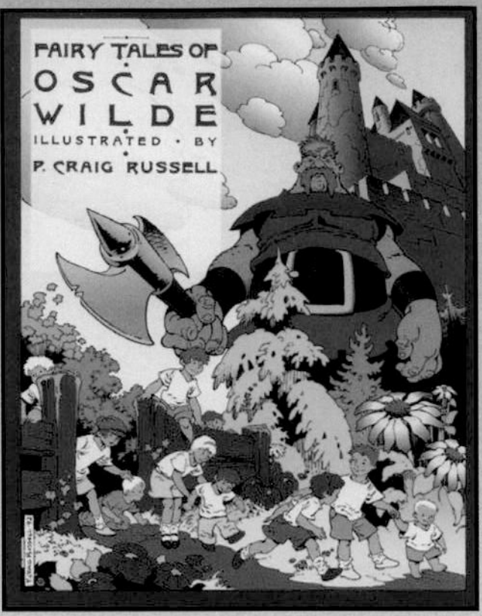
FAIRY TALES OF
OSCAR
WILDE
ILLUSTRATED · BY
P. CRAIG RUSSELL

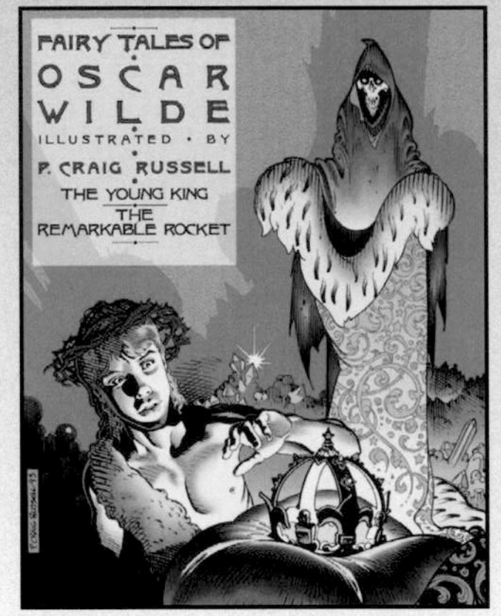
FAIRY TALES OF
OSCAR
WILDE
ILLUSTRATED · BY
P. CRAIG RUSSELL
THE YOUNG KING
THE
REMARKABLE ROCKET

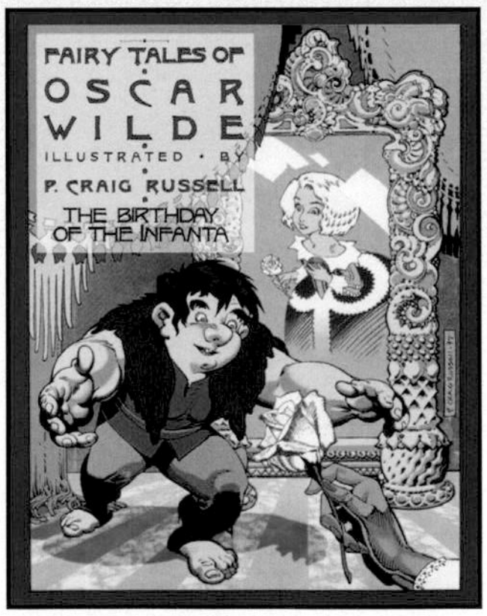
FAIRY TALES OF
OSCAR
WILDE
ILLUSTRATED · BY
P. CRAIG RUSSELL
THE BIRTHDAY
OF THE INFANTA

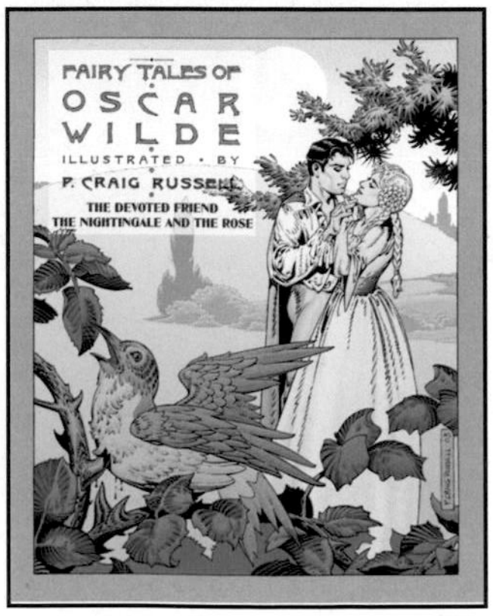
FAIRY TALES OF
OSCAR
WILDE
ILLUSTRATED · BY
P. CRAIG RUSSELL
THE DEVOTED FRIEND
THE NIGHTINGALE AND THE ROSE

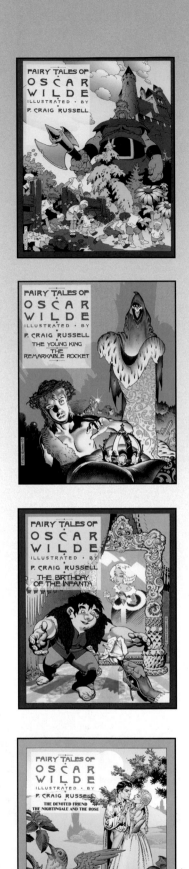

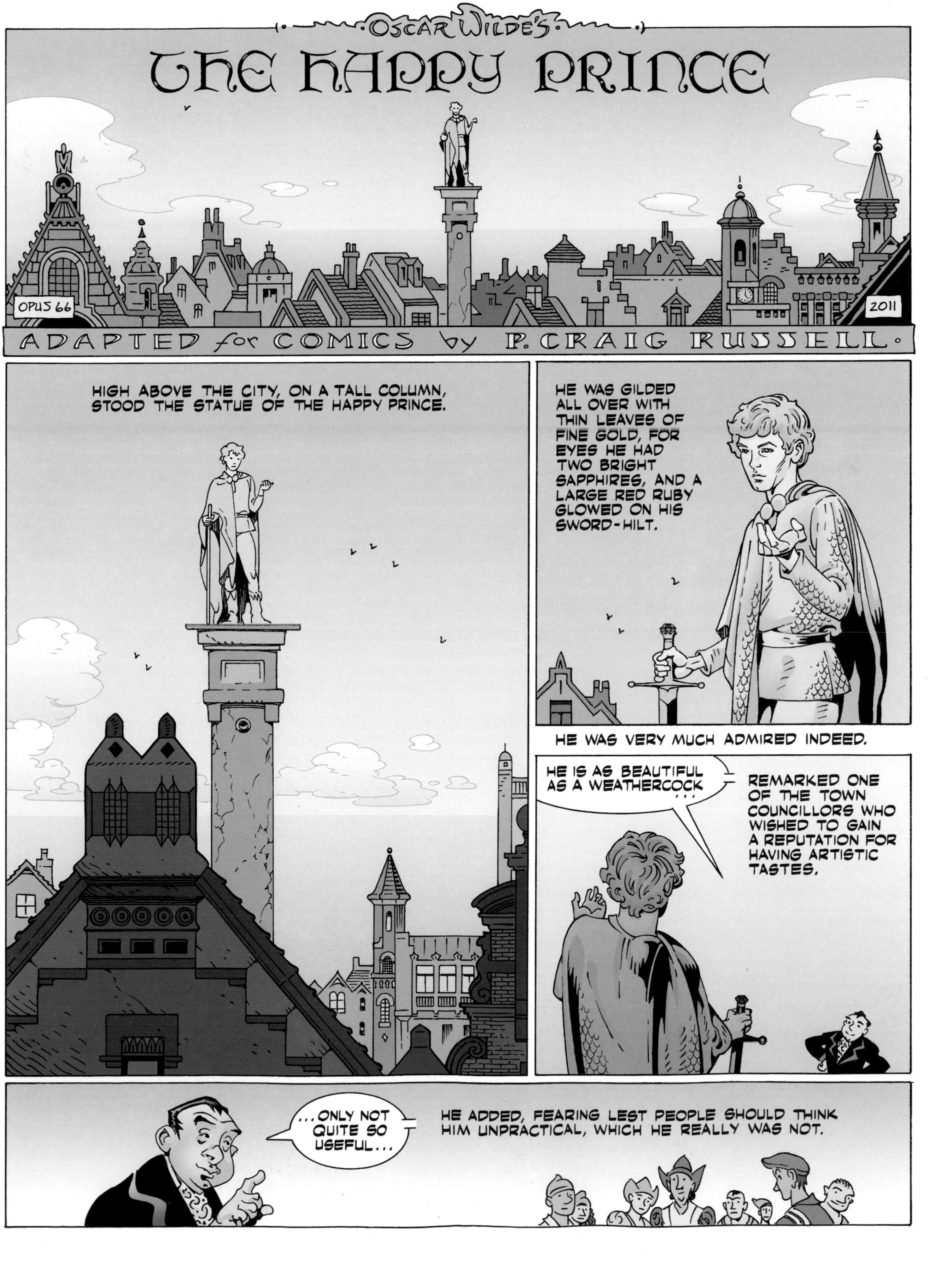

OSCAR WILDE'S
THE HAPPY PRINCE
OPUS 66
2011
ADAPTED for COMICS by P. CRAIG RUSSELL.
HIGH ABOVE THE CITY, ON A TALL COLUMN, STOOD THE STATUE OF THE HAPPY PRINCE.
HE WAS GILDED ALL OVER WITH THIN LEAVES OF FINE GOLD, FOR EYES HE HAD TWO BRIGHT SAPPHIRES, AND A LARGE RED RUBY GLOWED ON HIS SWORD-HILT.
HE WAS VERY MUCH ADMIRED INDEED.
HE IS AS BEAUTIFUL AS A WEATHERCOCK...
REMARKED ONE OF THE TOWN COUNCILLORS WHO WISHED TO GAIN A REPUTATION FOR HAVING ARTISTIC TASTES.
...ONLY NOT QUITE SO USEFUL...
HE ADDED, FEARING LEST PEOPLE SHOULD THINK HIM UNPRACTICAL, WHICH HE REALLY WAS NOT.

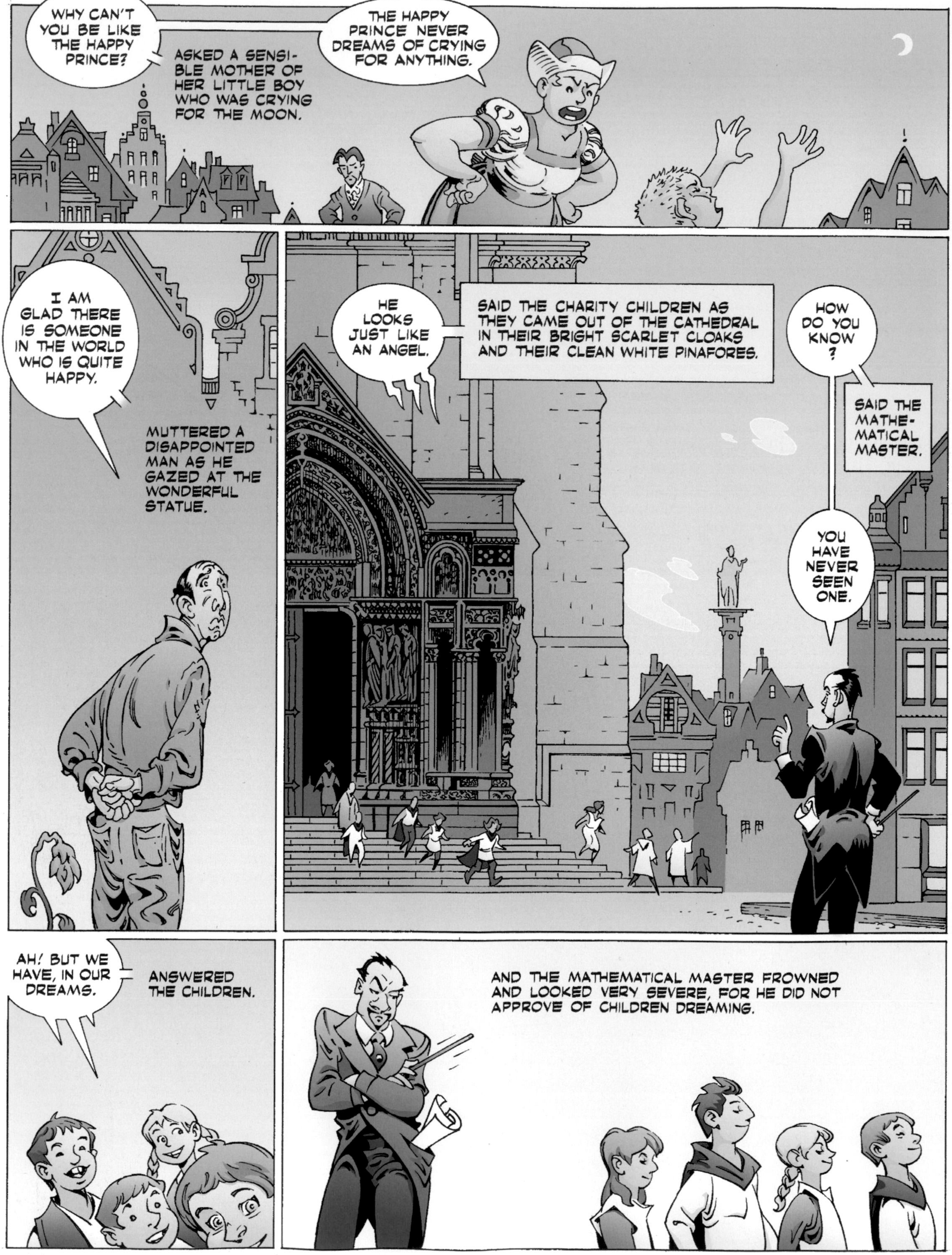

WHY CAN'T YOU BE LIKE THE HAPPY PRINCE?
ASKED A SENSIBLE MOTHER OF HER LITTLE BOY WHO WAS CRYING FOR THE MOON.
THE HAPPY PRINCE NEVER DREAMS OF CRYING FOR ANYTHING.
I AM GLAD THERE IS SOMEONE IN THE WORLD WHO IS QUITE HAPPY.
MUTTERED A DISAPPOINTED MAN AS HE GAZED AT THE WONDERFUL STATUE.
HE LOOKS JUST LIKE AN ANGEL.
SAID THE CHARITY CHILDREN AS THEY CAME OUT OF THE CATHEDRAL IN THEIR BRIGHT SCARLET CLOAKS AND THEIR CLEAN WHITE PINAFORES.
HOW DO YOU KNOW?
SAID THE MATHEMATICAL MASTER.
YOU HAVE NEVER SEEN ONE.
AH! BUT WE HAVE, IN OUR DREAMS.
ANSWERED THE CHILDREN.
AND THE MATHEMATICAL MASTER FROWNED AND LOOKED VERY SEVERE, FOR HE DID NOT APPROVE OF CHILDREN DREAMING.

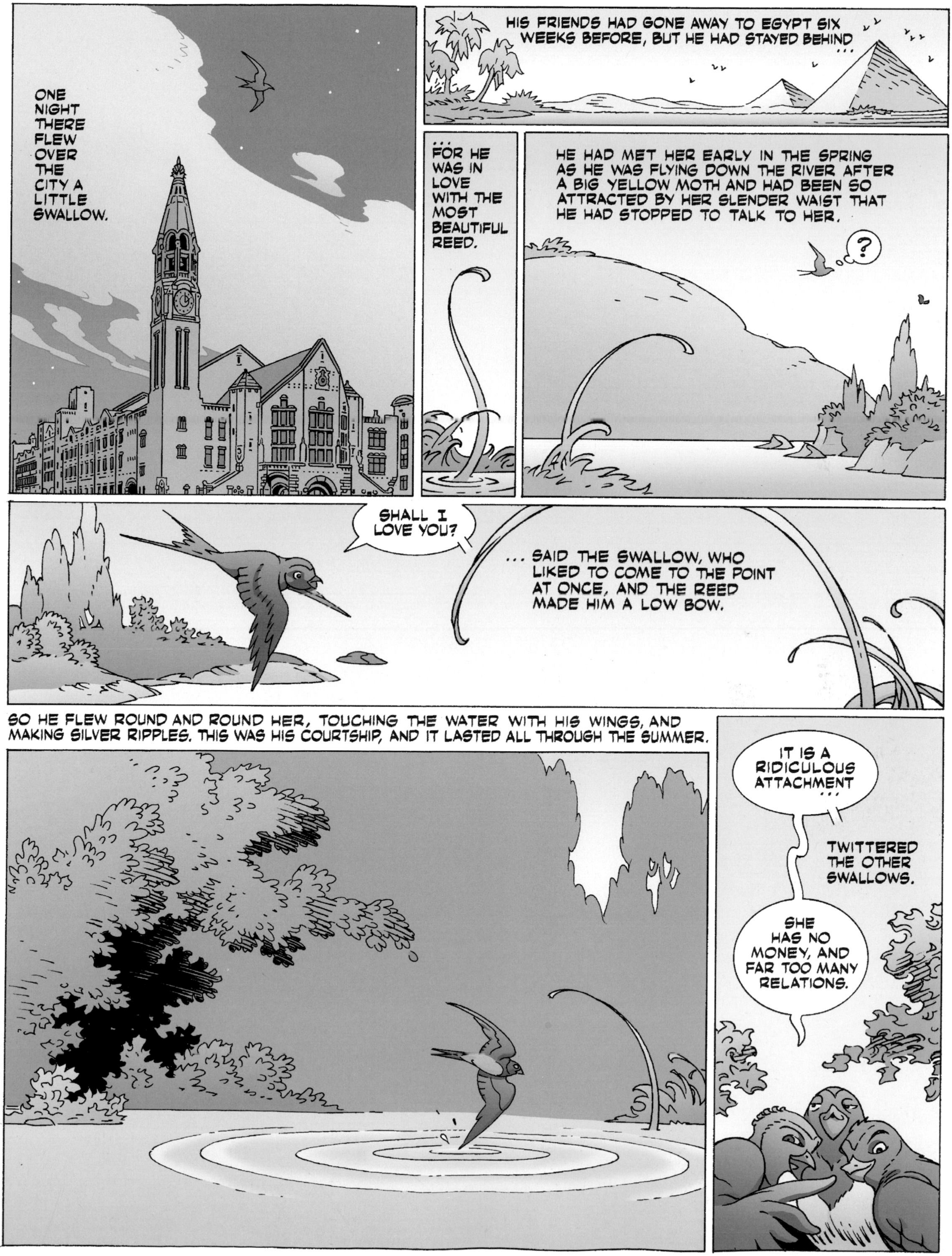
ONE NIGHT THERE FLEW OVER THE CITY A LITTLE SWALLOW.
HIS FRIENDS HAD GONE AWAY TO EGYPT SIX WEEKS BEFORE, BUT HE HAD STAYED BEHIND ...
... FOR HE WAS IN LOVE WITH THE MOST BEAUTIFUL REED.
HE HAD MET HER EARLY IN THE SPRING AS HE WAS FLYING DOWN THE RIVER AFTER A BIG YELLOW MOTH AND HAD BEEN SO ATTRACTED BY HER SLENDER WAIST THAT HE HAD STOPPED TO TALK TO HER.
?
SHALL I LOVE YOU?
... SAID THE SWALLOW, WHO LIKED TO COME TO THE POINT AT ONCE, AND THE REED MADE HIM A LOW BOW.
SO HE FLEW ROUND AND ROUND HER, TOUCHING THE WATER WITH HIS WINGS, AND MAKING SILVER RIPPLES. THIS WAS HIS COURTSHIP, AND IT LASTED ALL THROUGH THE SUMMER.
IT IS A RIDICULOUS ATTACHMENT ...
TWITTERED THE OTHER SWALLOWS.
SHE HAS NO MONEY, AND FAR TOO MANY RELATIONS.

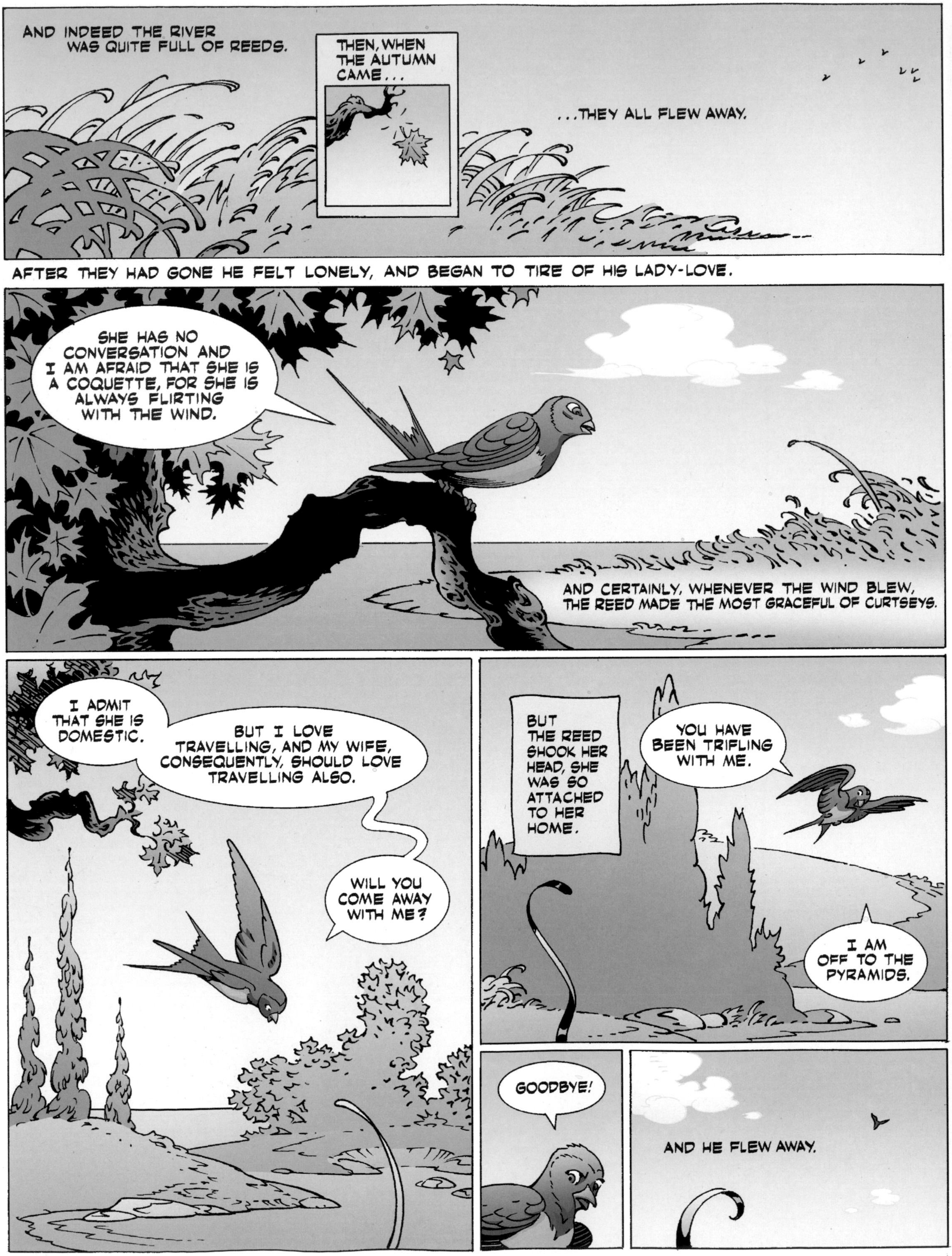
AND INDEED THE RIVER WAS QUITE FULL OF REEDS.
THEN, WHEN THE AUTUMN CAME...
...THEY ALL FLEW AWAY.
AFTER THEY HAD GONE HE FELT LONELY, AND BEGAN TO TIRE OF HIS LADY-LOVE.
SHE HAS NO CONVERSATION AND I AM AFRAID THAT SHE IS A COQUETTE, FOR SHE IS ALWAYS FLIRTING WITH THE WIND.
AND CERTAINLY, WHENEVER THE WIND BLEW, THE REED MADE THE MOST GRACEFUL OF CURTSEYS.
I ADMIT THAT SHE IS DOMESTIC.
BUT I LOVE TRAVELLING, AND MY WIFE, CONSEQUENTLY, SHOULD LOVE TRAVELLING ALSO.
WILL YOU COME AWAY WITH ME?
BUT THE REED SHOOK HER HEAD, SHE WAS SO ATTACHED TO HER HOME.
YOU HAVE BEEN TRIFLING WITH ME.
I AM OFF TO THE PYRAMIDS.
GOODBYE!
AND HE FLEW AWAY.

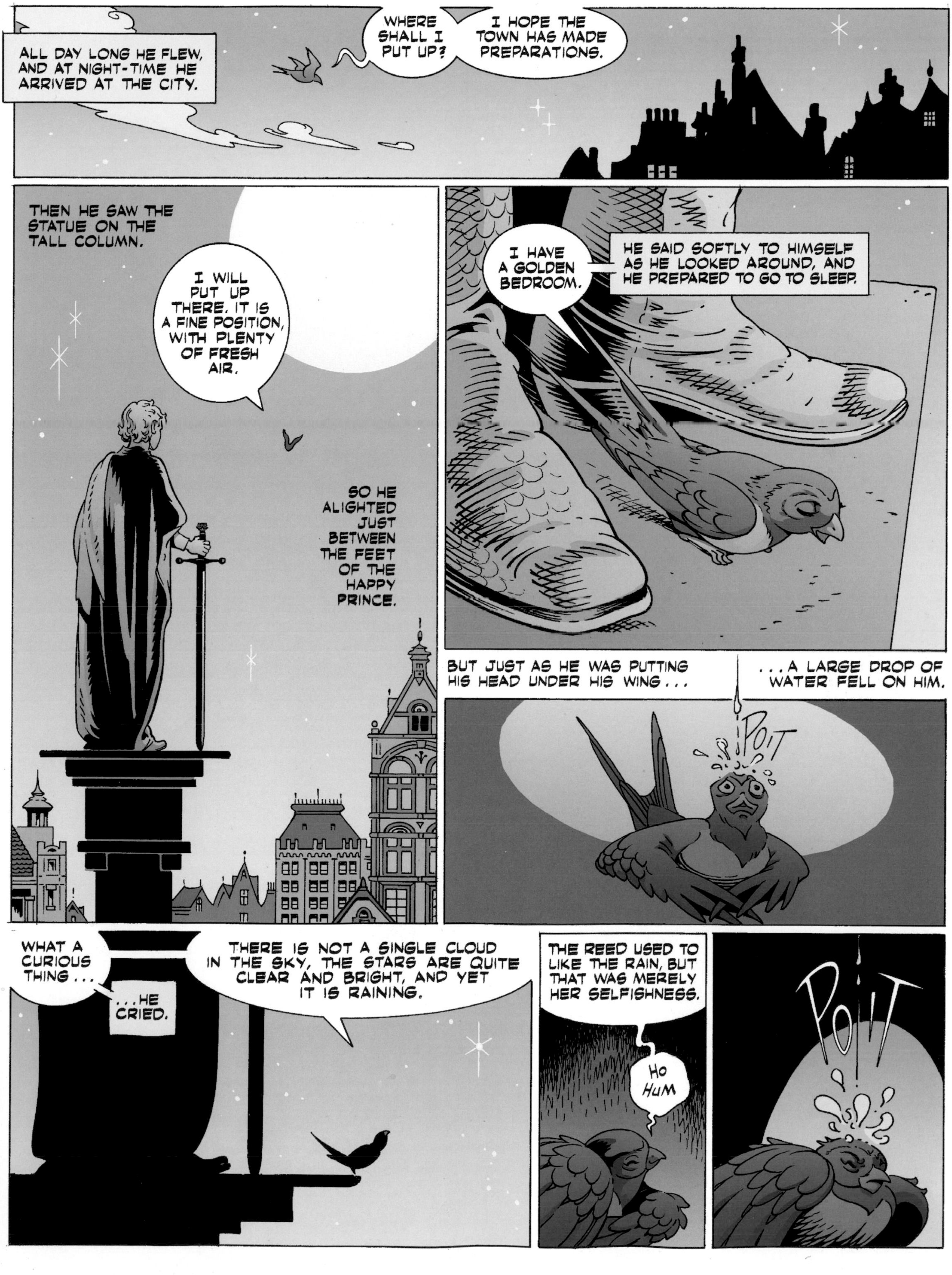
ALL DAY LONG HE FLEW, AND AT NIGHT-TIME HE ARRIVED AT THE CITY.
WHERE SHALL I PUT UP?
I HOPE THE TOWN HAS MADE PREPARATIONS.
THEN HE SAW THE STATUE ON THE TALL COLUMN.
I WILL PUT UP THERE. IT IS A FINE POSITION, WITH PLENTY OF FRESH AIR.
SO HE ALIGHTED JUST BETWEEN THE FEET OF THE HAPPY PRINCE.
I HAVE A GOLDEN BEDROOM.
HE SAID SOFTLY TO HIMSELF AS HE LOOKED AROUND, AND HE PREPARED TO GO TO SLEEP.
BUT JUST AS HE WAS PUTTING HIS HEAD UNDER HIS WING . . .
. . . A LARGE DROP OF WATER FELL ON HIM.
POIT
WHAT A CURIOUS THING . . .
. . . HE CRIED.
THERE IS NOT A SINGLE CLOUD IN THE SKY, THE STARS ARE QUITE CLEAR AND BRIGHT, AND YET IT IS RAINING.
THE REED USED TO LIKE THE RAIN, BUT THAT WAS MERELY HER SELFISHNESS.
HO HUM
POIT

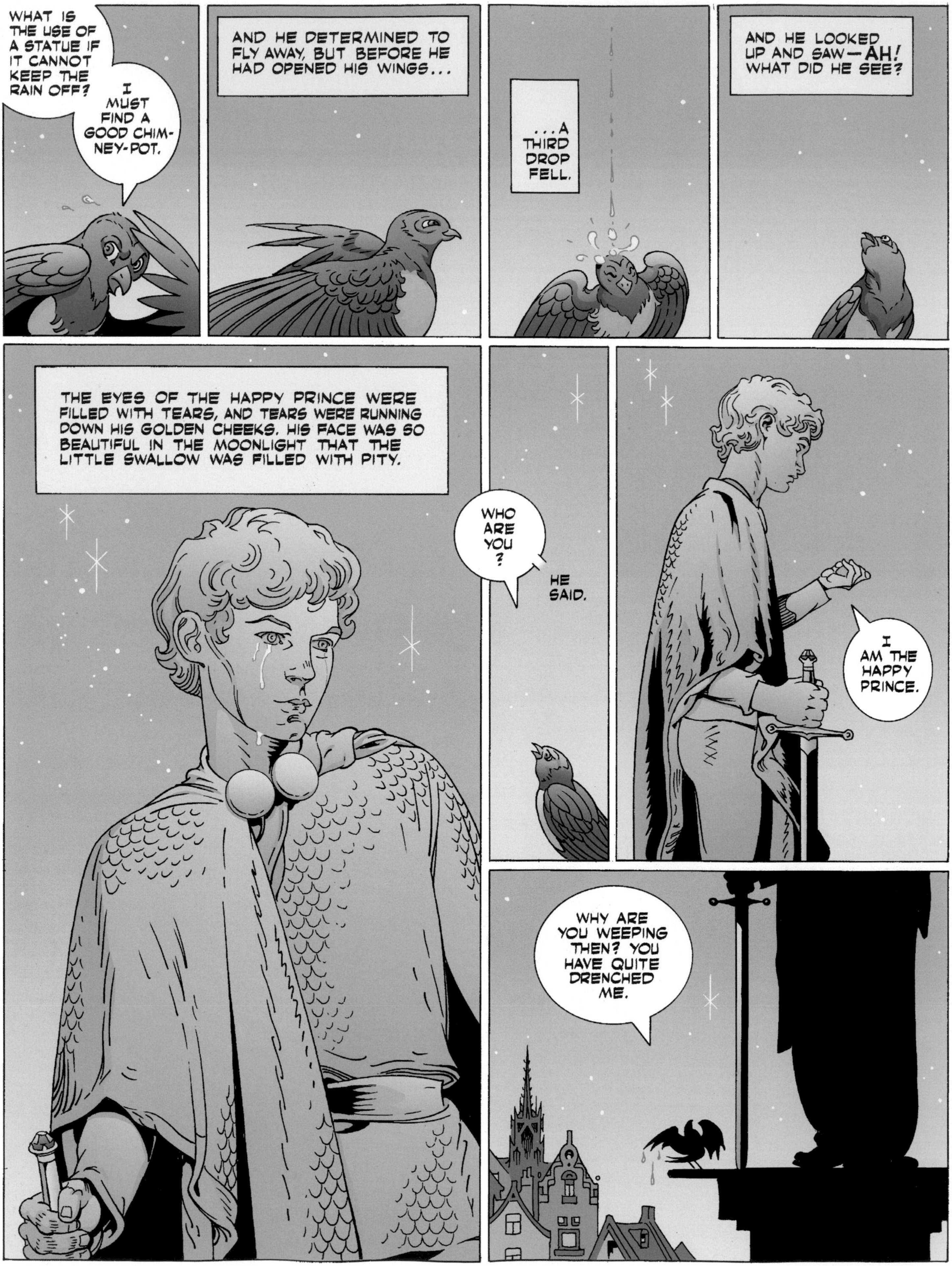
WHAT IS THE USE OF A STATUE IF IT CANNOT KEEP THE RAIN OFF?
I MUST FIND A GOOD CHIMNEY-POT.
AND HE DETERMINED TO FLY AWAY, BUT BEFORE HE HAD OPENED HIS WINGS...
...A THIRD DROP FELL.
AND HE LOOKED UP AND SAW—AH! WHAT DID HE SEE?
THE EYES OF THE HAPPY PRINCE WERE FILLED WITH TEARS, AND TEARS WERE RUNNING DOWN HIS GOLDEN CHEEKS. HIS FACE WAS SO BEAUTIFUL IN THE MOONLIGHT THAT THE LITTLE SWALLOW WAS FILLED WITH PITY.
WHO ARE YOU?
HE SAID.
I AM THE HAPPY PRINCE.
WHY ARE YOU WEEPING THEN? YOU HAVE QUITE DRENCHED ME.

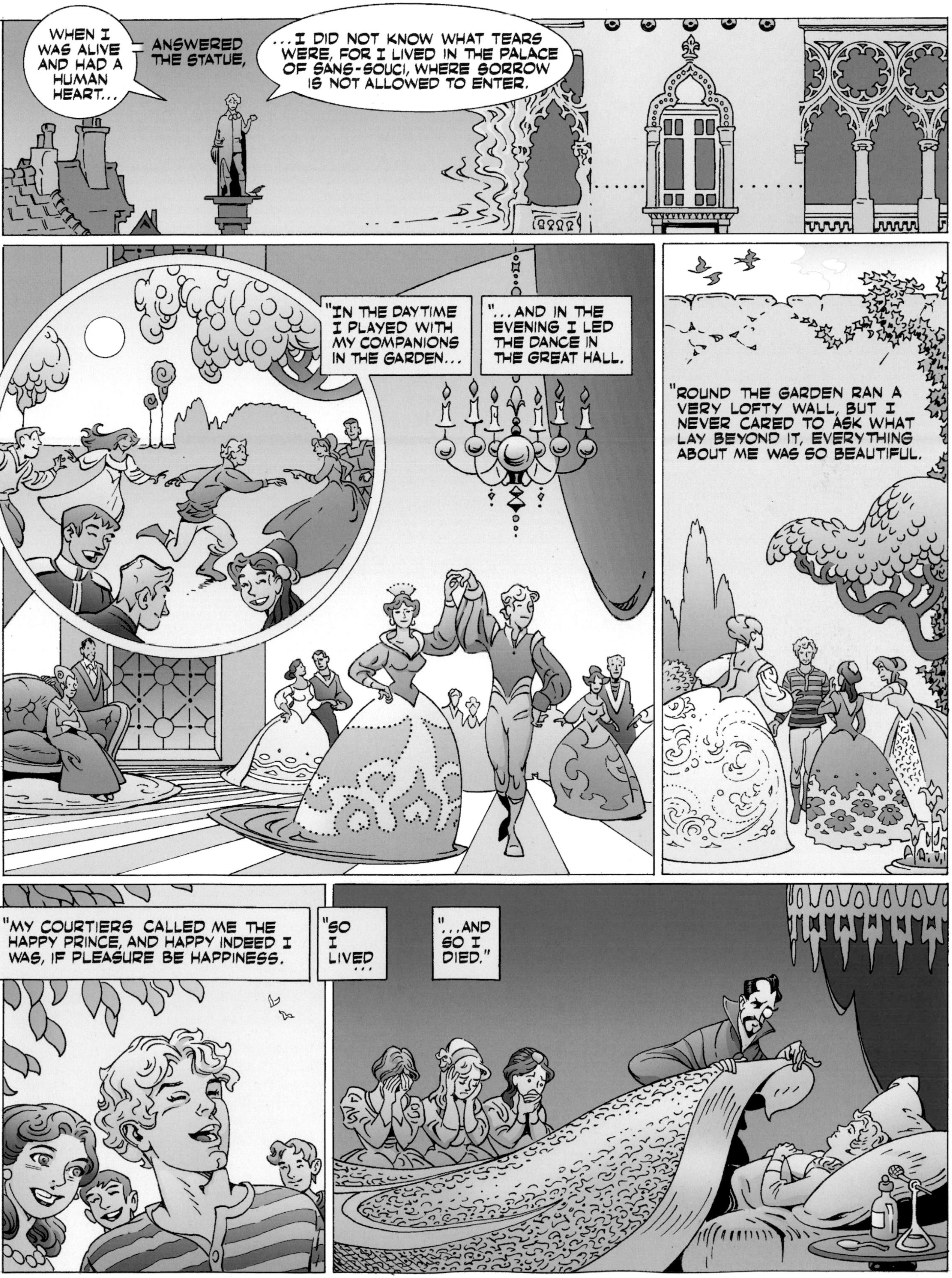
WHEN I WAS ALIVE AND HAD A HUMAN HEART...
— ANSWERED THE STATUE,
...I DID NOT KNOW WHAT TEARS WERE, FOR I LIVED IN THE PALACE OF SANS-SOUCI, WHERE SORROW IS NOT ALLOWED TO ENTER.
"IN THE DAYTIME I PLAYED WITH MY COMPANIONS IN THE GARDEN...
"...AND IN THE EVENING I LED THE DANCE IN THE GREAT HALL.
"ROUND THE GARDEN RAN A VERY LOFTY WALL, BUT I NEVER CARED TO ASK WHAT LAY BEYOND IT, EVERYTHING ABOUT ME WAS SO BEAUTIFUL.
"MY COURTIERS CALLED ME THE HAPPY PRINCE, AND HAPPY INDEED I WAS, IF PLEASURE BE HAPPINESS.
"SO I LIVED...
"...AND SO I DIED."

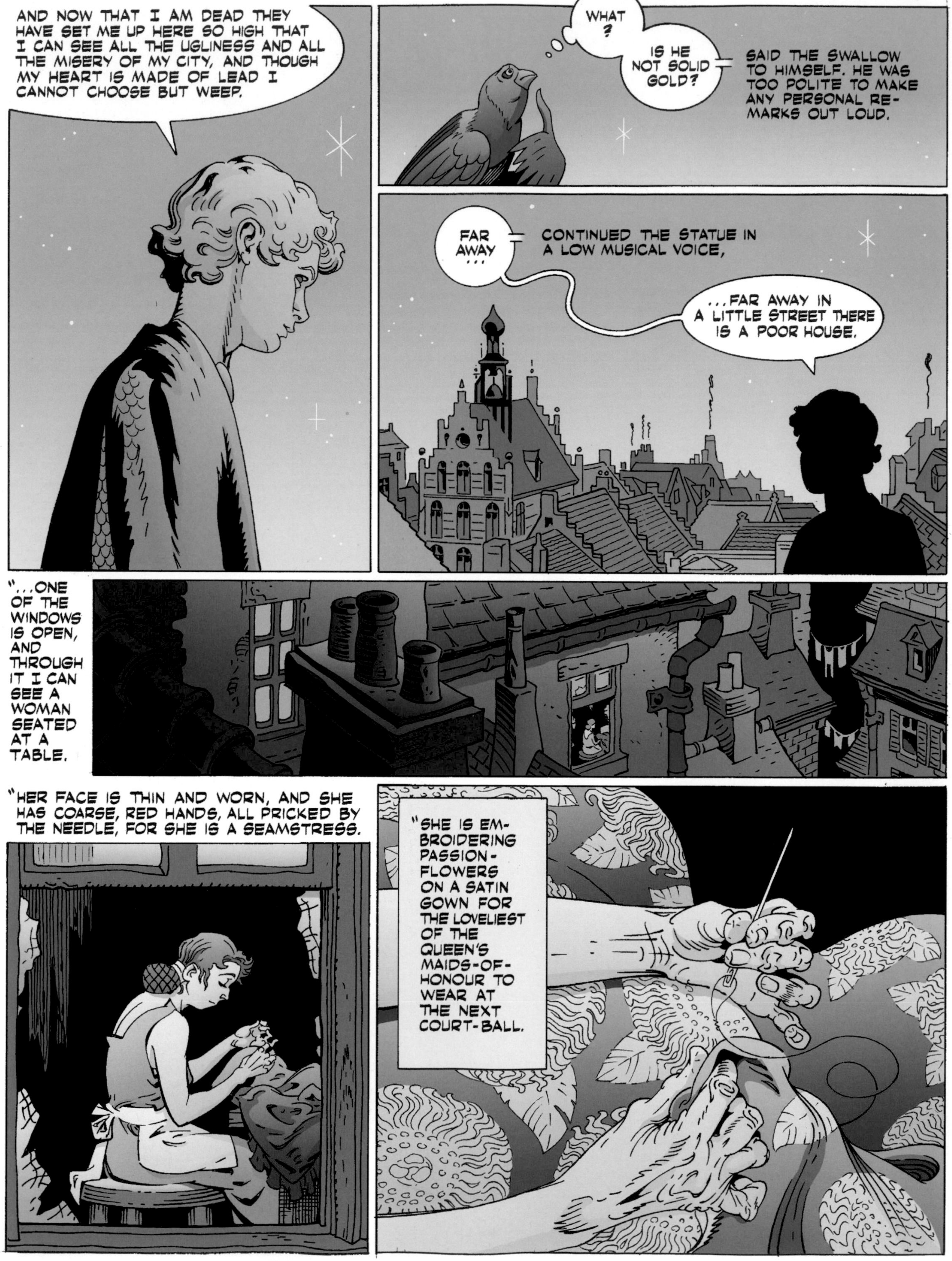
AND NOW THAT I AM DEAD THEY HAVE SET ME UP HERE SO HIGH THAT I CAN SEE ALL THE UGLINESS AND ALL THE MISERY OF MY CITY, AND THOUGH MY HEART IS MADE OF LEAD I CANNOT CHOOSE BUT WEEP.
WHAT?
IS HE NOT SOLID GOLD?
SAID THE SWALLOW TO HIMSELF. HE WAS TOO POLITE TO MAKE ANY PERSONAL RE-MARKS OUT LOUD.
FAR AWAY...
CONTINUED THE STATUE IN A LOW MUSICAL VOICE,
...FAR AWAY IN A LITTLE STREET THERE IS A POOR HOUSE.
"...ONE OF THE WINDOWS IS OPEN, AND THROUGH IT I CAN SEE A WOMAN SEATED AT A TABLE.
"HER FACE IS THIN AND WORN, AND SHE HAS COARSE, RED HANDS, ALL PRICKED BY THE NEEDLE, FOR SHE IS A SEAMSTRESS.
"SHE IS EM-BROIDERING PASSION-FLOWERS ON A SATIN GOWN FOR THE LOVELIEST OF THE QUEEN'S MAIDS-OF-HONOUR TO WEAR AT THE NEXT COURT-BALL.

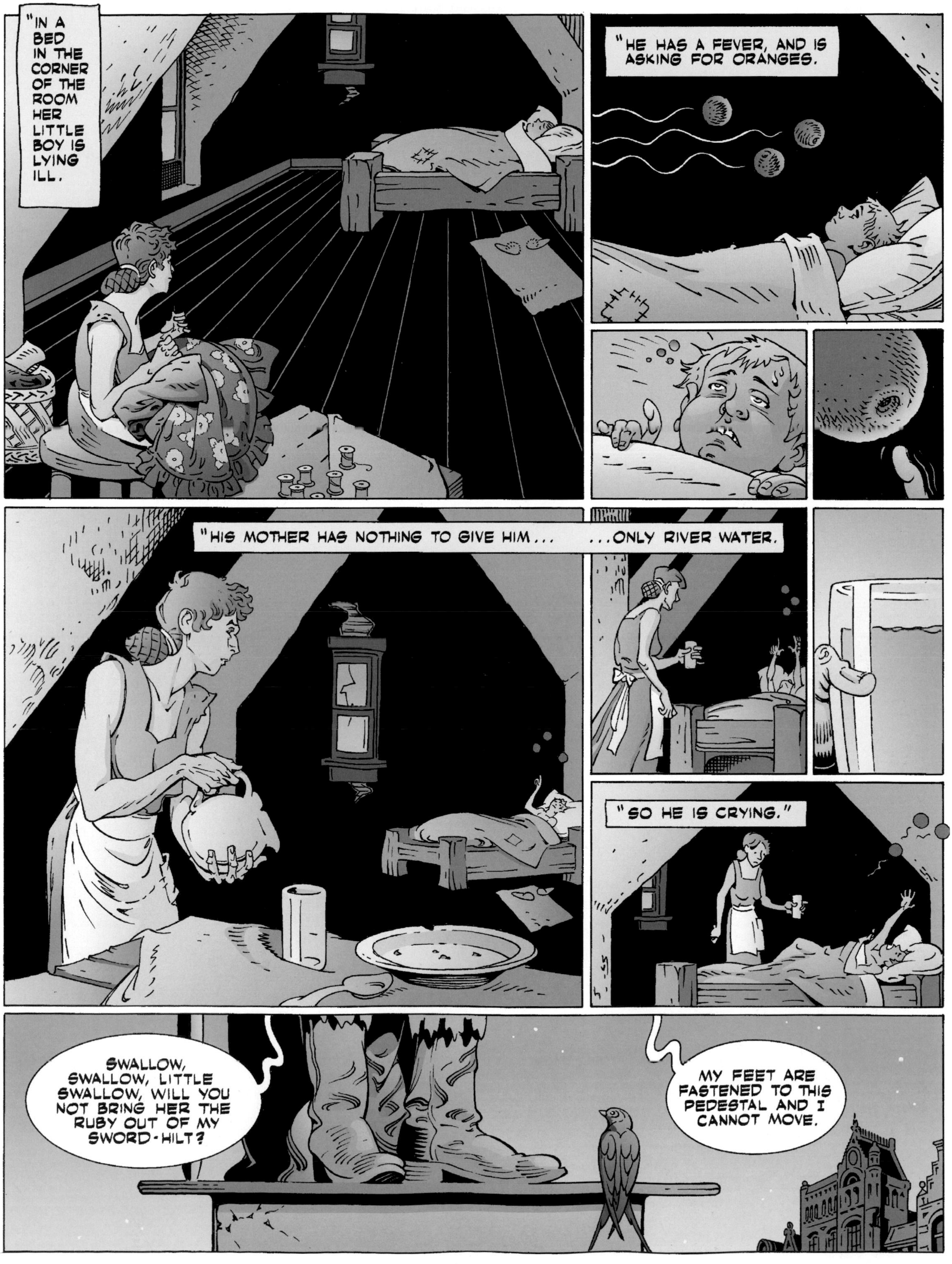
"IN A BED IN THE CORNER OF THE ROOM HER LITTLE BOY IS LYING ILL.
"HE HAS A FEVER, AND IS ASKING FOR ORANGES.
"HIS MOTHER HAS NOTHING TO GIVE HIM...
...ONLY RIVER WATER.
"SO HE IS CRYING."
SWALLOW, SWALLOW, LITTLE SWALLOW, WILL YOU NOT BRING HER THE RUBY OUT OF MY SWORD-HILT?
MY FEET ARE FASTENED TO THIS PEDESTAL AND I CANNOT MOVE.

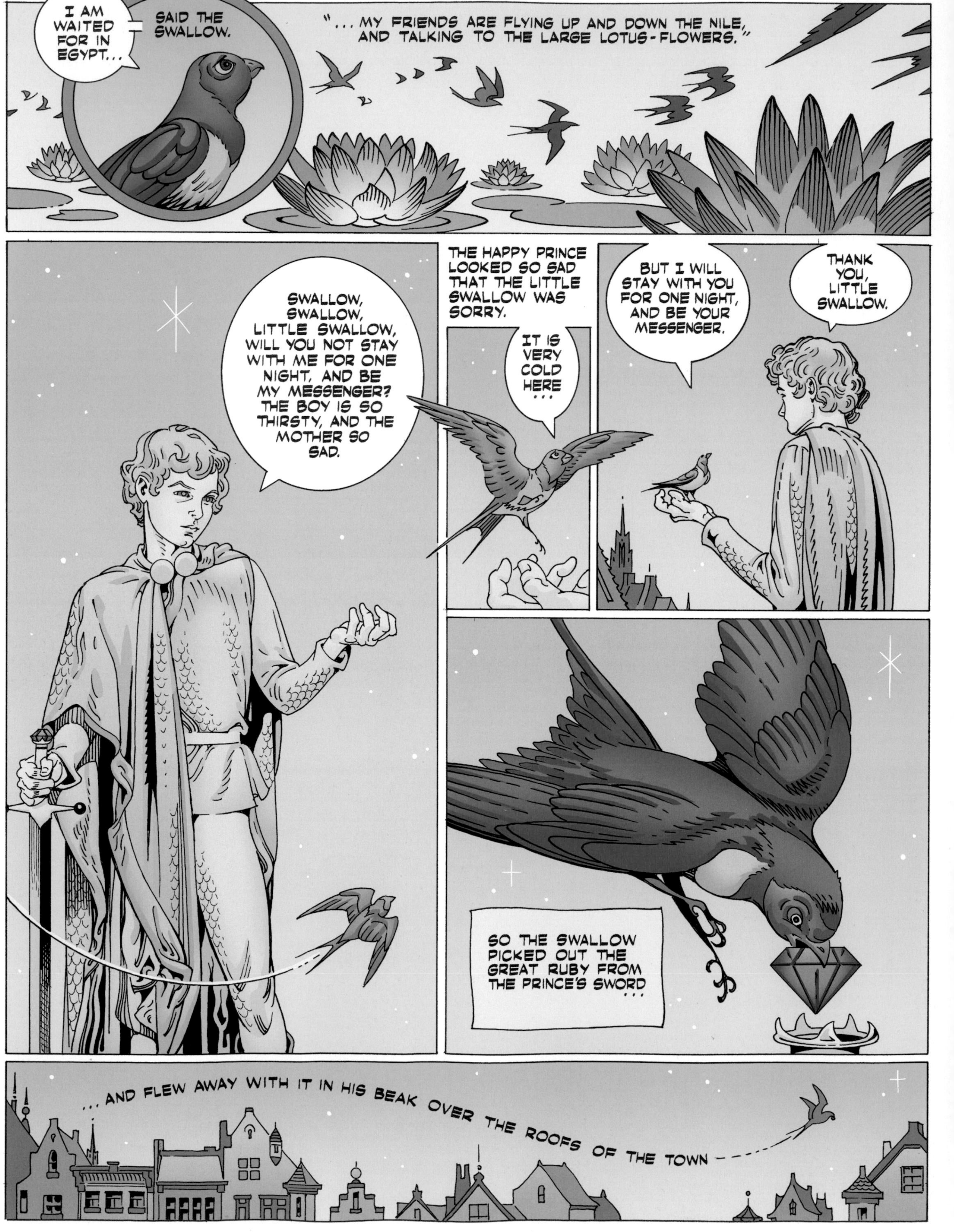
I AM WAITED FOR IN EGYPT...
SAID THE SWALLOW.
"... MY FRIENDS ARE FLYING UP AND DOWN THE NILE, AND TALKING TO THE LARGE LOTUS-FLOWERS."
SWALLOW, SWALLOW, LITTLE SWALLOW, WILL YOU NOT STAY WITH ME FOR ONE NIGHT, AND BE MY MESSENGER? THE BOY IS SO THIRSTY, AND THE MOTHER SO SAD.
THE HAPPY PRINCE LOOKED SO SAD THAT THE LITTLE SWALLOW WAS SORRY.
IT IS VERY COLD HERE ...
BUT I WILL STAY WITH YOU FOR ONE NIGHT, AND BE YOUR MESSENGER.
THANK YOU, LITTLE SWALLOW.
SO THE SWALLOW PICKED OUT THE GREAT RUBY FROM THE PRINCE'S SWORD ...
... AND FLEW AWAY WITH IT IN HIS BEAK OVER THE ROOFS OF THE TOWN

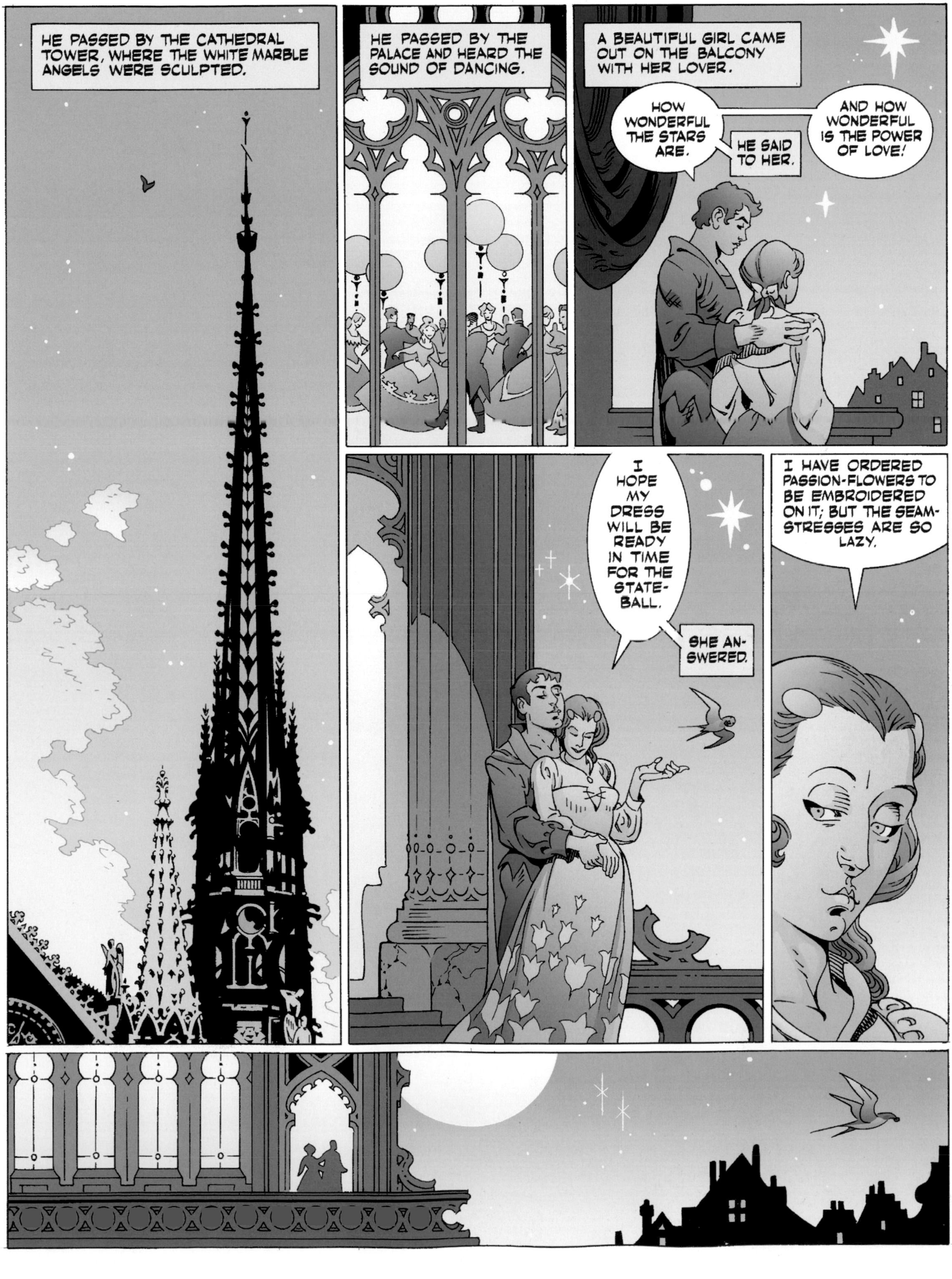
HE PASSED BY THE CATHEDRAL TOWER, WHERE THE WHITE MARBLE ANGELS WERE SCULPTED.
HE PASSED BY THE PALACE AND HEARD THE SOUND OF DANCING.
A BEAUTIFUL GIRL CAME OUT ON THE BALCONY WITH HER LOVER.
HOW WONDERFUL THE STARS ARE.
HE SAID TO HER.
AND HOW WONDERFUL IS THE POWER OF LOVE!
I HOPE MY DRESS WILL BE READY IN TIME FOR THE STATE-BALL.
SHE ANSWERED.
I HAVE ORDERED PASSION-FLOWERS TO BE EMBROIDERED ON IT; BUT THE SEAMSTRESSES ARE SO LAZY.

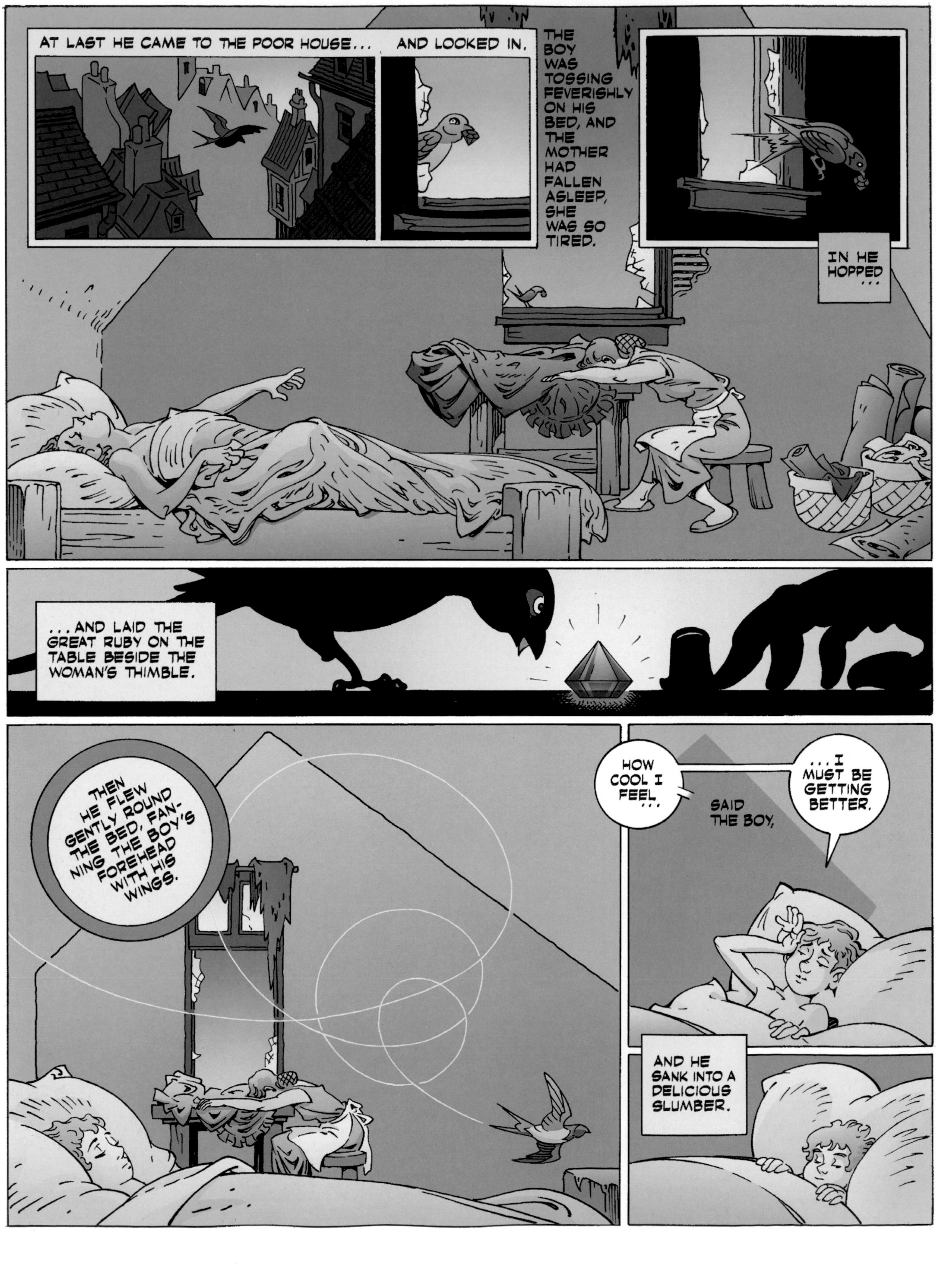
AT LAST HE CAME TO THE POOR HOUSE...
AND LOOKED IN.
THE BOY WAS TOSSING FEVERISHLY ON HIS BED, AND THE MOTHER HAD FALLEN ASLEEP, SHE WAS SO TIRED.
IN HE HOPPED...
...AND LAID THE GREAT RUBY ON THE TABLE BESIDE THE WOMAN'S THIMBLE.
THEN HE FLEW GENTLY ROUND THE BED, FANNING THE BOY'S FOREHEAD WITH HIS WINGS.
HOW COOL I FEEL...
SAID THE BOY,
...I MUST BE GETTING BETTER.
AND HE SANK INTO A DELICIOUS SLUMBER.

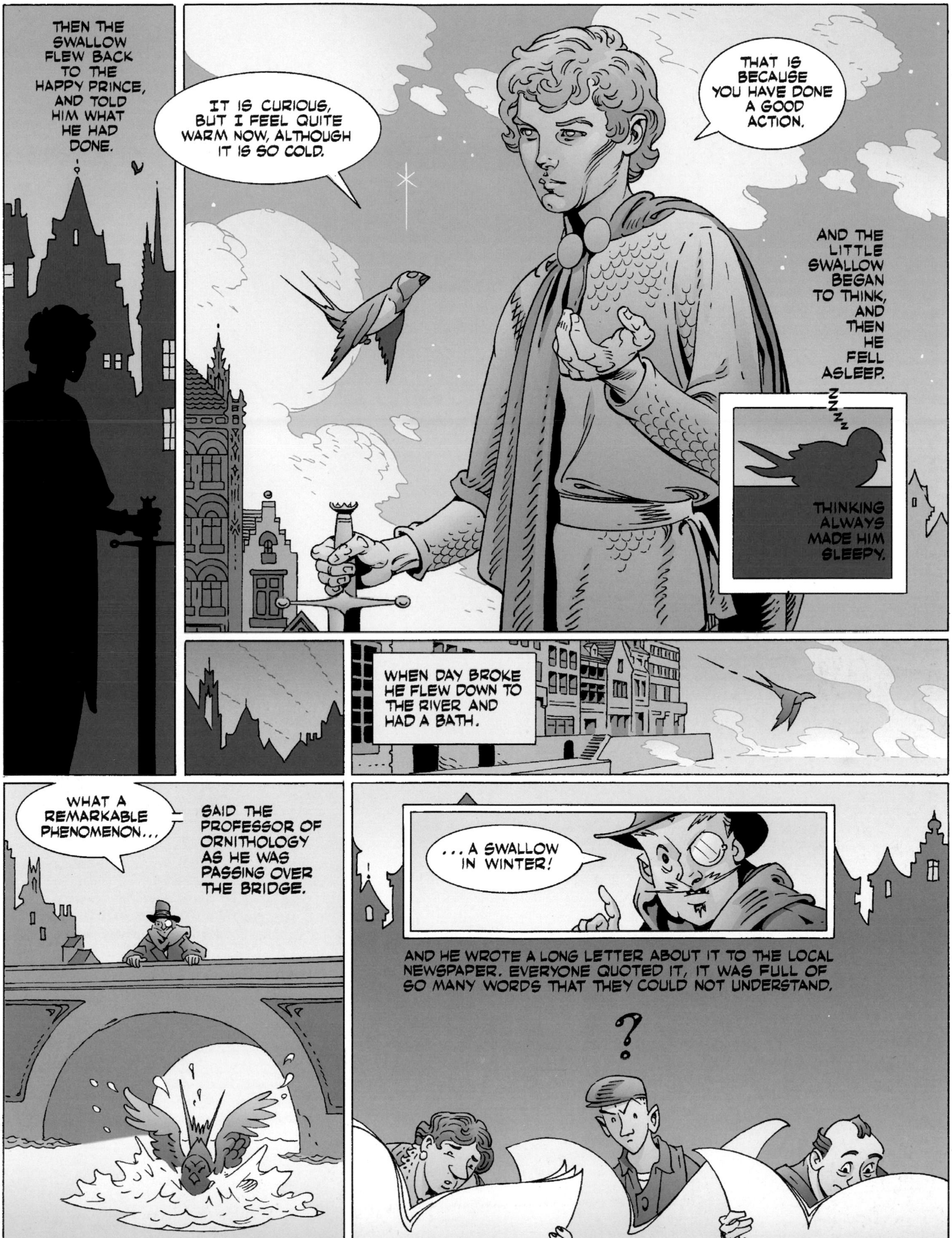
THEN THE SWALLOW FLEW BACK TO THE HAPPY PRINCE, AND TOLD HIM WHAT HE HAD DONE.
IT IS CURIOUS, BUT I FEEL QUITE WARM NOW, ALTHOUGH IT IS SO COLD.
THAT IS BECAUSE YOU HAVE DONE A GOOD ACTION.
AND THE LITTLE SWALLOW BEGAN TO THINK, AND THEN HE FELL ASLEEP.
ZZZZ
THINKING ALWAYS MADE HIM SLEEPY.
WHEN DAY BROKE HE FLEW DOWN TO THE RIVER AND HAD A BATH.
WHAT A REMARKABLE PHENOMENON...
SAID THE PROFESSOR OF ORNITHOLOGY AS HE WAS PASSING OVER THE BRIDGE.
...A SWALLOW IN WINTER!
AND HE WROTE A LONG LETTER ABOUT IT TO THE LOCAL NEWSPAPER. EVERYONE QUOTED IT, IT WAS FULL OF SO MANY WORDS THAT THEY COULD NOT UNDERSTAND.
?

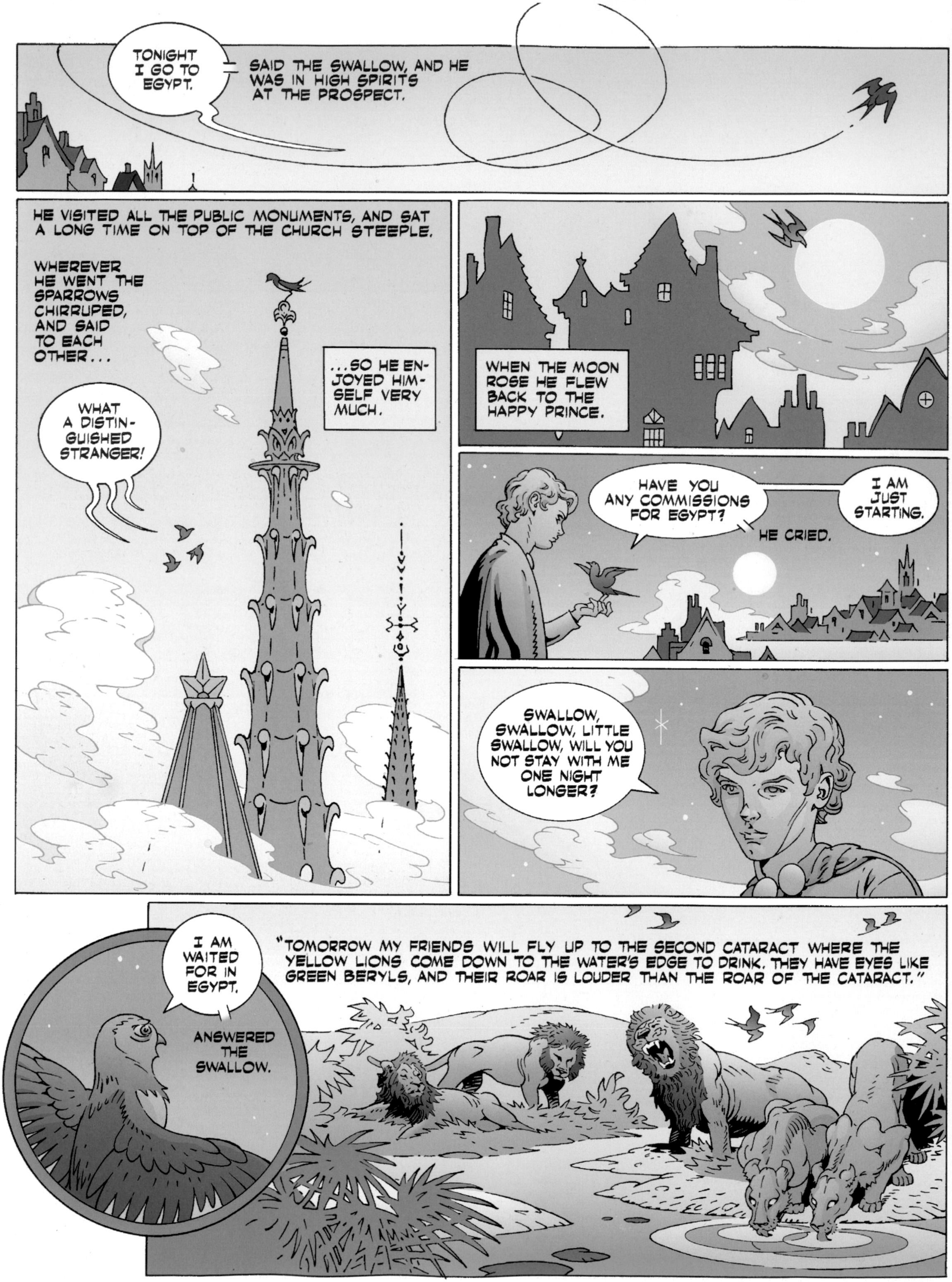
TONIGHT I GO TO EGYPT.
SAID THE SWALLOW, AND HE WAS IN HIGH SPIRITS AT THE PROSPECT.
HE VISITED ALL THE PUBLIC MONUMENTS, AND SAT A LONG TIME ON TOP OF THE CHURCH STEEPLE.
WHEREVER HE WENT THE SPARROWS CHIRRUPED, AND SAID TO EACH OTHER...
WHAT A DISTINGUISHED STRANGER!
...SO HE ENJOYED HIMSELF VERY MUCH.
WHEN THE MOON ROSE HE FLEW BACK TO THE HAPPY PRINCE.
HAVE YOU ANY COMMISSIONS FOR EGYPT?
I AM JUST STARTING.
HE CRIED.
SWALLOW, SWALLOW, LITTLE SWALLOW, WILL YOU NOT STAY WITH ME ONE NIGHT LONGER?
I AM WAITED FOR IN EGYPT.
ANSWERED THE SWALLOW.
"TOMORROW MY FRIENDS WILL FLY UP TO THE SECOND CATARACT WHERE THE YELLOW LIONS COME DOWN TO THE WATER'S EDGE TO DRINK. THEY HAVE EYES LIKE GREEN BERYLS, AND THEIR ROAR IS LOUDER THAN THE ROAR OF THE CATARACT."

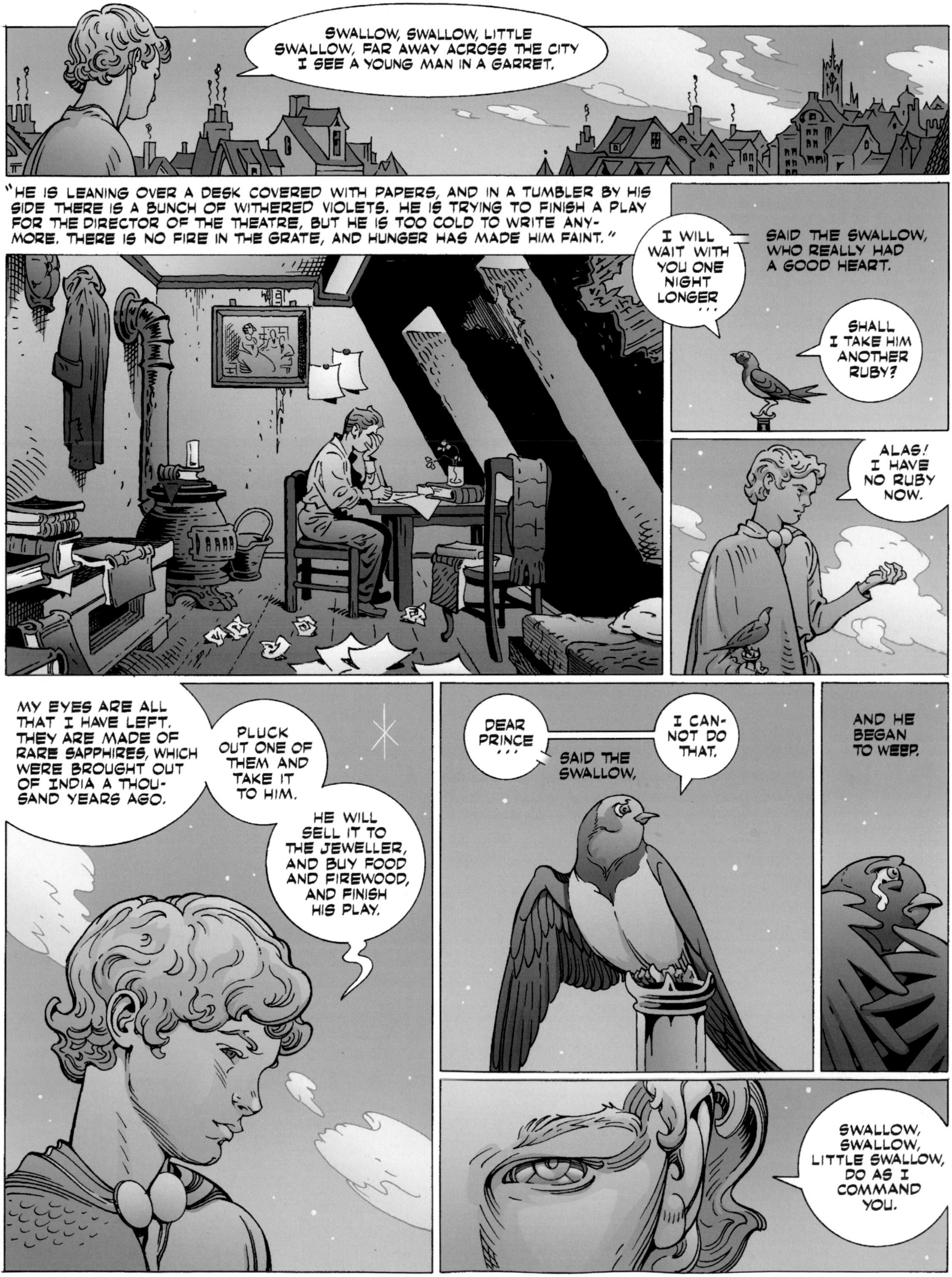
SWALLOW, SWALLOW, LITTLE SWALLOW, FAR AWAY ACROSS THE CITY I SEE A YOUNG MAN IN A GARRET.
"HE IS LEANING OVER A DESK COVERED WITH PAPERS, AND IN A TUMBLER BY HIS SIDE THERE IS A BUNCH OF WITHERED VIOLETS. HE IS TRYING TO FINISH A PLAY FOR THE DIRECTOR OF THE THEATRE, BUT HE IS TOO COLD TO WRITE ANY-MORE. THERE IS NO FIRE IN THE GRATE, AND HUNGER HAS MADE HIM FAINT."
I WILL WAIT WITH YOU ONE NIGHT LONGER . . .
SAID THE SWALLOW, WHO REALLY HAD A GOOD HEART.
SHALL I TAKE HIM ANOTHER RUBY?
ALAS! I HAVE NO RUBY NOW.
MY EYES ARE ALL THAT I HAVE LEFT. THEY ARE MADE OF RARE SAPPHIRES, WHICH WERE BROUGHT OUT OF INDIA A THOU-SAND YEARS AGO.
PLUCK OUT ONE OF THEM AND TAKE IT TO HIM.
HE WILL SELL IT TO THE JEWELLER, AND BUY FOOD AND FIREWOOD, AND FINISH HIS PLAY.
DEAR PRINCE . . .
SAID THE SWALLOW,
I CAN-NOT DO THAT.
AND HE BEGAN TO WEEP.
SWALLOW, SWALLOW, LITTLE SWALLOW, DO AS I COMMAND YOU.

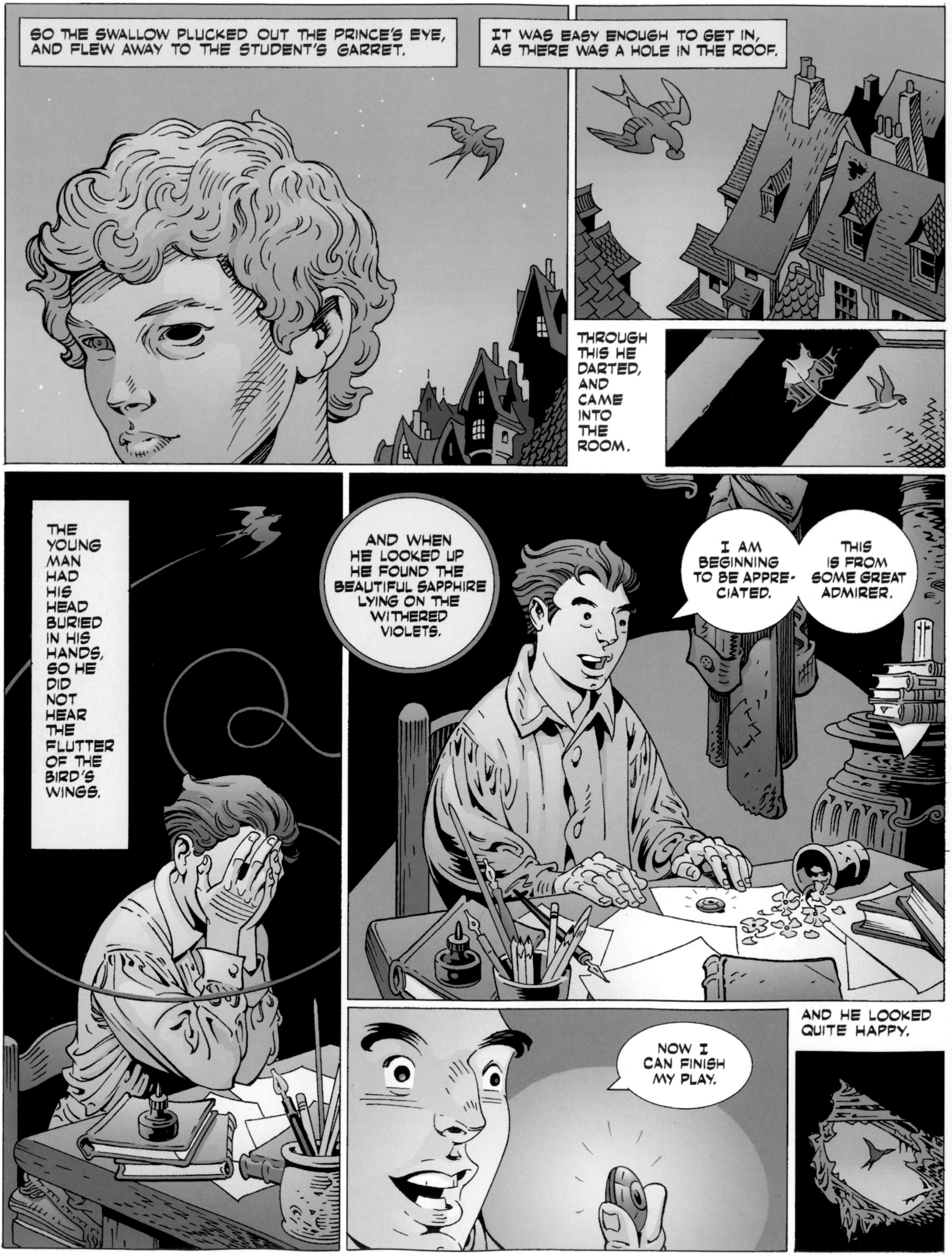
SO THE SWALLOW PLUCKED OUT THE PRINCE'S EYE, AND FLEW AWAY TO THE STUDENT'S GARRET.
IT WAS EASY ENOUGH TO GET IN, AS THERE WAS A HOLE IN THE ROOF.
THROUGH THIS HE DARTED, AND CAME INTO THE ROOM.
THE YOUNG MAN HAD HIS HEAD BURIED IN HIS HANDS, SO HE DID NOT HEAR THE FLUTTER OF THE BIRD'S WINGS.
AND WHEN HE LOOKED UP HE FOUND THE BEAUTIFUL SAPPHIRE LYING ON THE WITHERED VIOLETS.
I AM BEGINNING TO BE APPRE-CIATED.
THIS IS FROM SOME GREAT ADMIRER.
NOW I CAN FINISH MY PLAY.
AND HE LOOKED QUITE HAPPY.

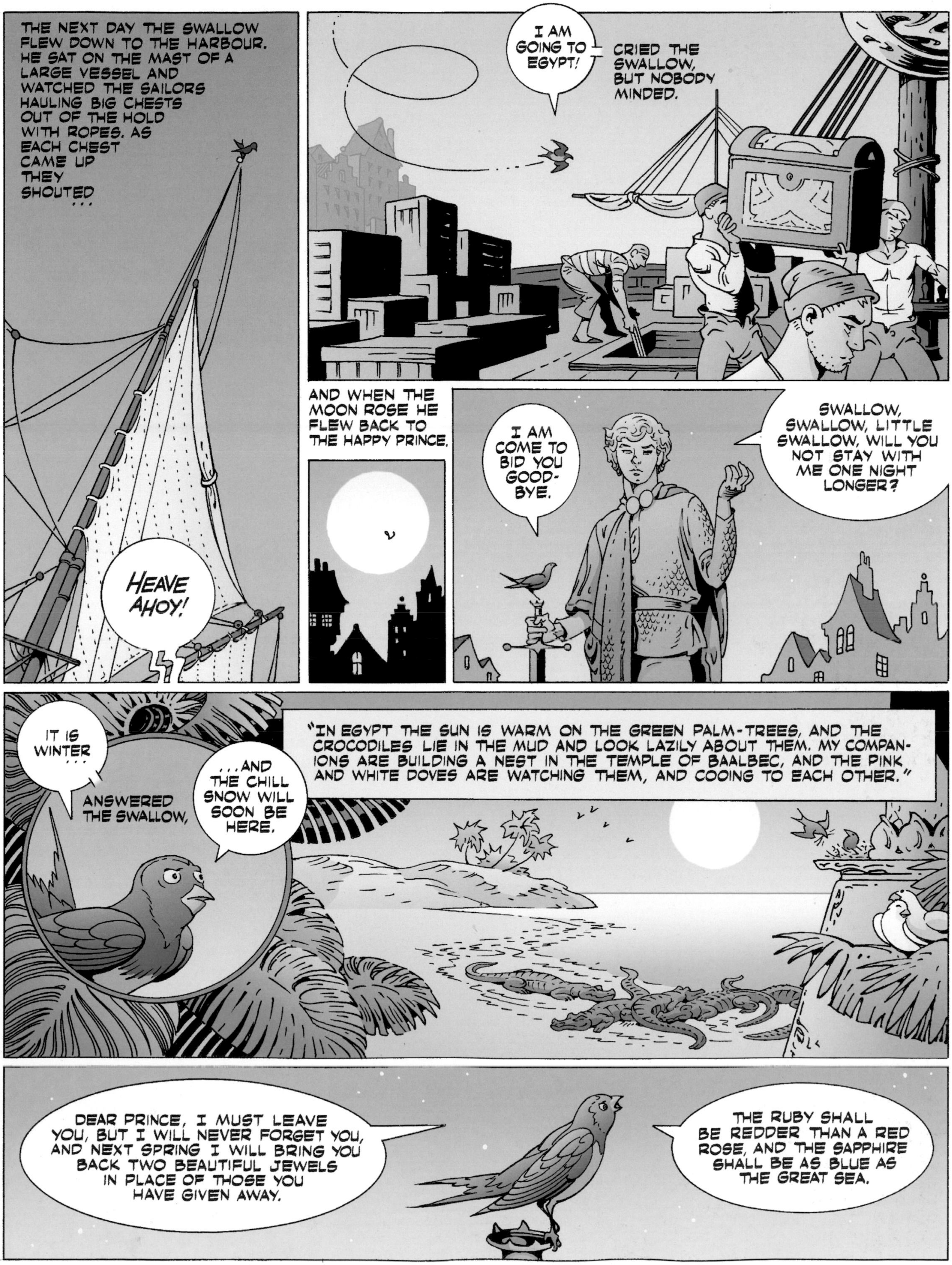
THE NEXT DAY THE SWALLOW FLEW DOWN TO THE HARBOUR. HE SAT ON THE MAST OF A LARGE VESSEL AND WATCHED THE SAILORS HAULING BIG CHESTS OUT OF THE HOLD WITH ROPES. AS EACH CHEST CAME UP THEY SHOUTED . . .
HEAVE AHOY!
I AM GOING TO EGYPT!
CRIED THE SWALLOW, BUT NOBODY MINDED.
AND WHEN THE MOON ROSE HE FLEW BACK TO THE HAPPY PRINCE.
I AM COME TO BID YOU GOOD-BYE.
SWALLOW, SWALLOW, LITTLE SWALLOW, WILL YOU NOT STAY WITH ME ONE NIGHT LONGER?
IT IS WINTER . . .
ANSWERED THE SWALLOW,
. . . AND THE CHILL SNOW WILL SOON BE HERE.
"IN EGYPT THE SUN IS WARM ON THE GREEN PALM-TREES, AND THE CROCODILES LIE IN THE MUD AND LOOK LAZILY ABOUT THEM. MY COMPANIONS ARE BUILDING A NEST IN THE TEMPLE OF BAALBEC, AND THE PINK AND WHITE DOVES ARE WATCHING THEM, AND COOING TO EACH OTHER."
DEAR PRINCE, I MUST LEAVE YOU, BUT I WILL NEVER FORGET YOU, AND NEXT SPRING I WILL BRING YOU BACK TWO BEAUTIFUL JEWELS IN PLACE OF THOSE YOU HAVE GIVEN AWAY.
THE RUBY SHALL BE REDDER THAN A RED ROSE, AND THE SAPPHIRE SHALL BE AS BLUE AS THE GREAT SEA.

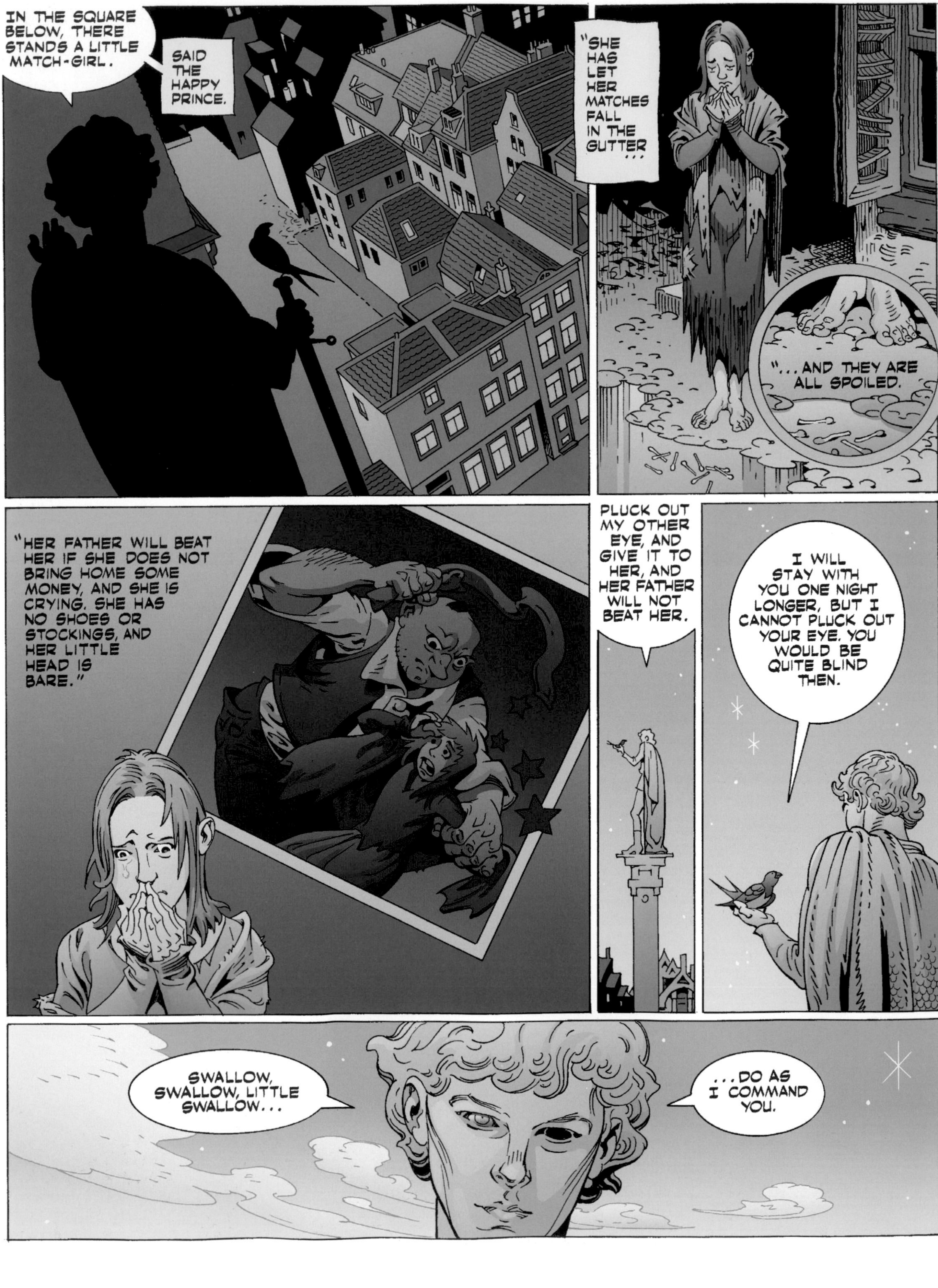
IN THE SQUARE BELOW, THERE STANDS A LITTLE MATCH-GIRL.
SAID THE HAPPY PRINCE.
"SHE HAS LET HER MATCHES FALL IN THE GUTTER...
"...AND THEY ARE ALL SPOILED.
"HER FATHER WILL BEAT HER IF SHE DOES NOT BRING HOME SOME MONEY, AND SHE IS CRYING. SHE HAS NO SHOES OR STOCKINGS, AND HER LITTLE HEAD IS BARE."
PLUCK OUT MY OTHER EYE, AND GIVE IT TO HER, AND HER FATHER WILL NOT BEAT HER.
I WILL STAY WITH YOU ONE NIGHT LONGER, BUT I CANNOT PLUCK OUT YOUR EYE. YOU WOULD BE QUITE BLIND THEN.
SWALLOW, SWALLOW, LITTLE SWALLOW...
...DO AS I COMMAND YOU.

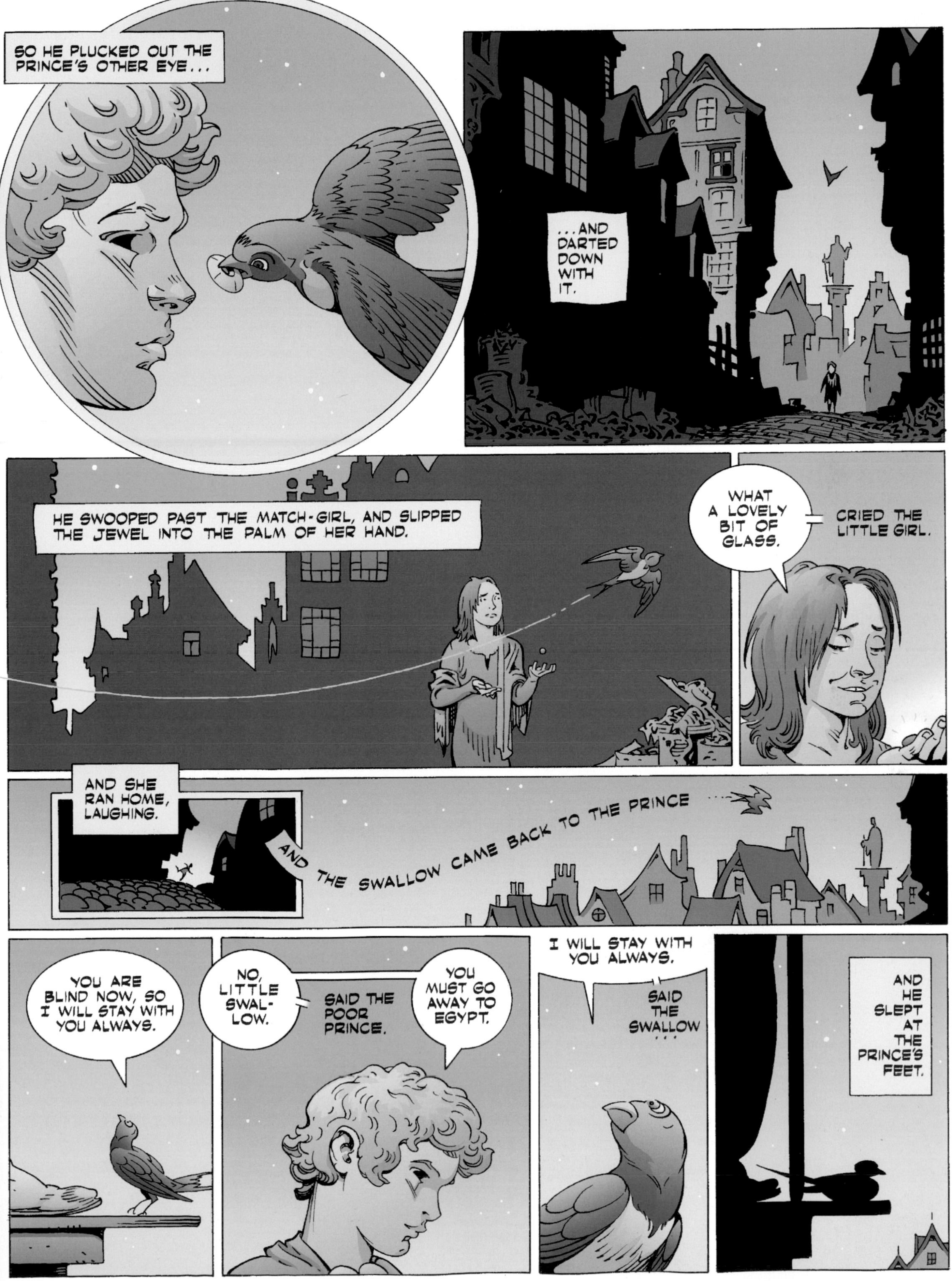
SO HE PLUCKED OUT THE PRINCE'S OTHER EYE...
...AND DARTED DOWN WITH IT.
HE SWOOPED PAST THE MATCH-GIRL, AND SLIPPED THE JEWEL INTO THE PALM OF HER HAND.
WHAT A LOVELY BIT OF GLASS.
CRIED THE LITTLE GIRL.
AND SHE RAN HOME, LAUGHING.
AND THE SWALLOW CAME BACK TO THE PRINCE
YOU ARE BLIND NOW, SO I WILL STAY WITH YOU ALWAYS.
NO, LITTLE SWAL-LOW.
SAID THE POOR PRINCE.
YOU MUST GO AWAY TO EGYPT.
I WILL STAY WITH YOU ALWAYS.
SAID THE SWALLOW...
AND HE SLEPT AT THE PRINCE'S FEET.

ALL THE NEXT DAY HE SAT ON THE PRINCE'S SHOULDER AND TOLD HIM STORIES OF WHAT HE HAD SEEN IN STRANGE LANDS.

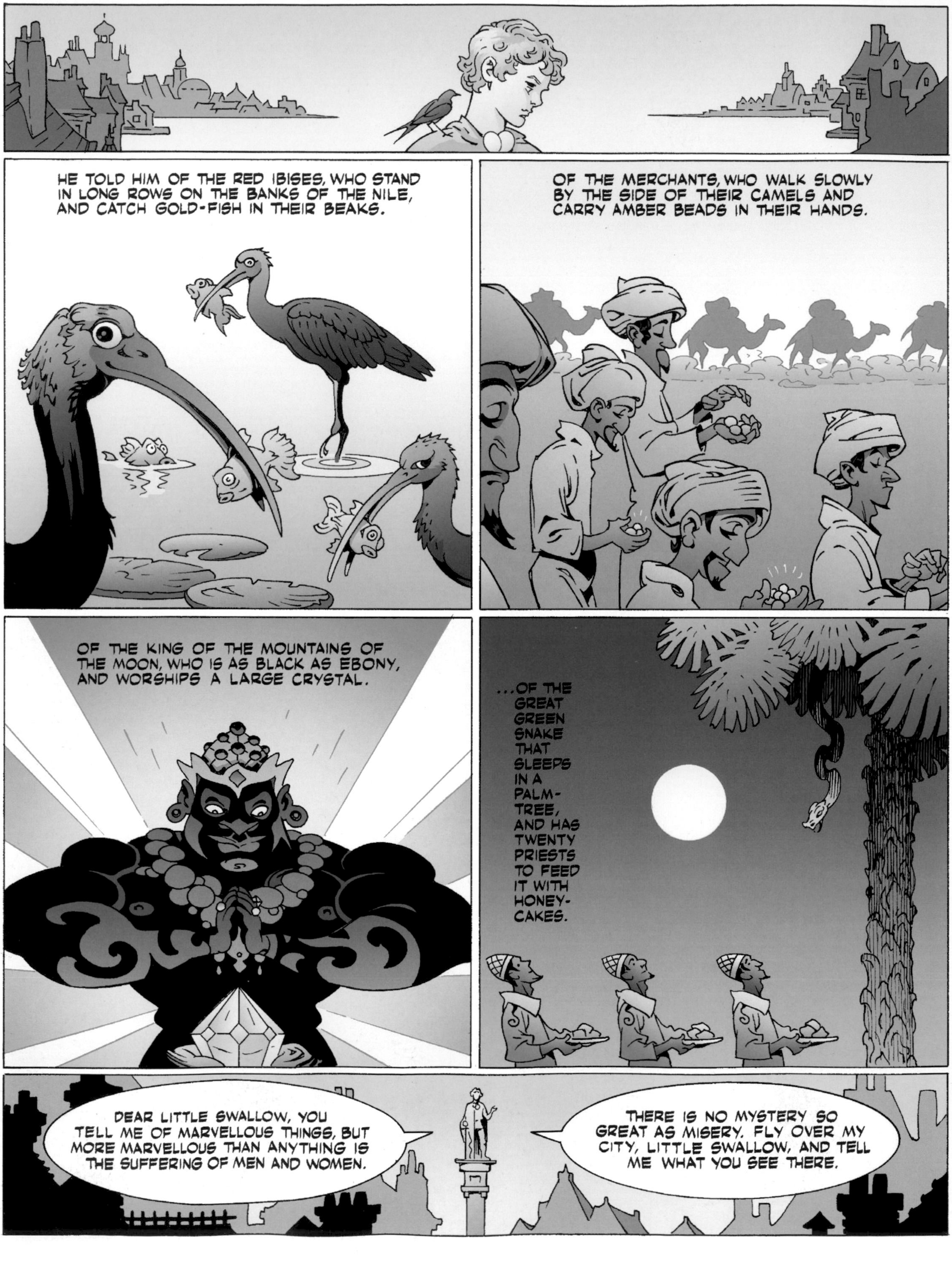
HE TOLD HIM OF THE RED IBISES, WHO STAND IN LONG ROWS ON THE BANKS OF THE NILE, AND CATCH GOLD-FISH IN THEIR BEAKS.
OF THE MERCHANTS, WHO WALK SLOWLY BY THE SIDE OF THEIR CAMELS AND CARRY AMBER BEADS IN THEIR HANDS.
OF THE KING OF THE MOUNTAINS OF THE MOON, WHO IS AS BLACK AS EBONY, AND WORSHIPS A LARGE CRYSTAL.
...OF THE GREAT GREEN SNAKE THAT SLEEPS IN A PALM-TREE, AND HAS TWENTY PRIESTS TO FEED IT WITH HONEY-CAKES.
DEAR LITTLE SWALLOW, YOU TELL ME OF MARVELLOUS THINGS, BUT MORE MARVELLOUS THAN ANYTHING IS THE SUFFERING OF MEN AND WOMEN.
THERE IS NO MYSTERY SO GREAT AS MISERY. FLY OVER MY CITY, LITTLE SWALLOW, AND TELL ME WHAT YOU SEE THERE.

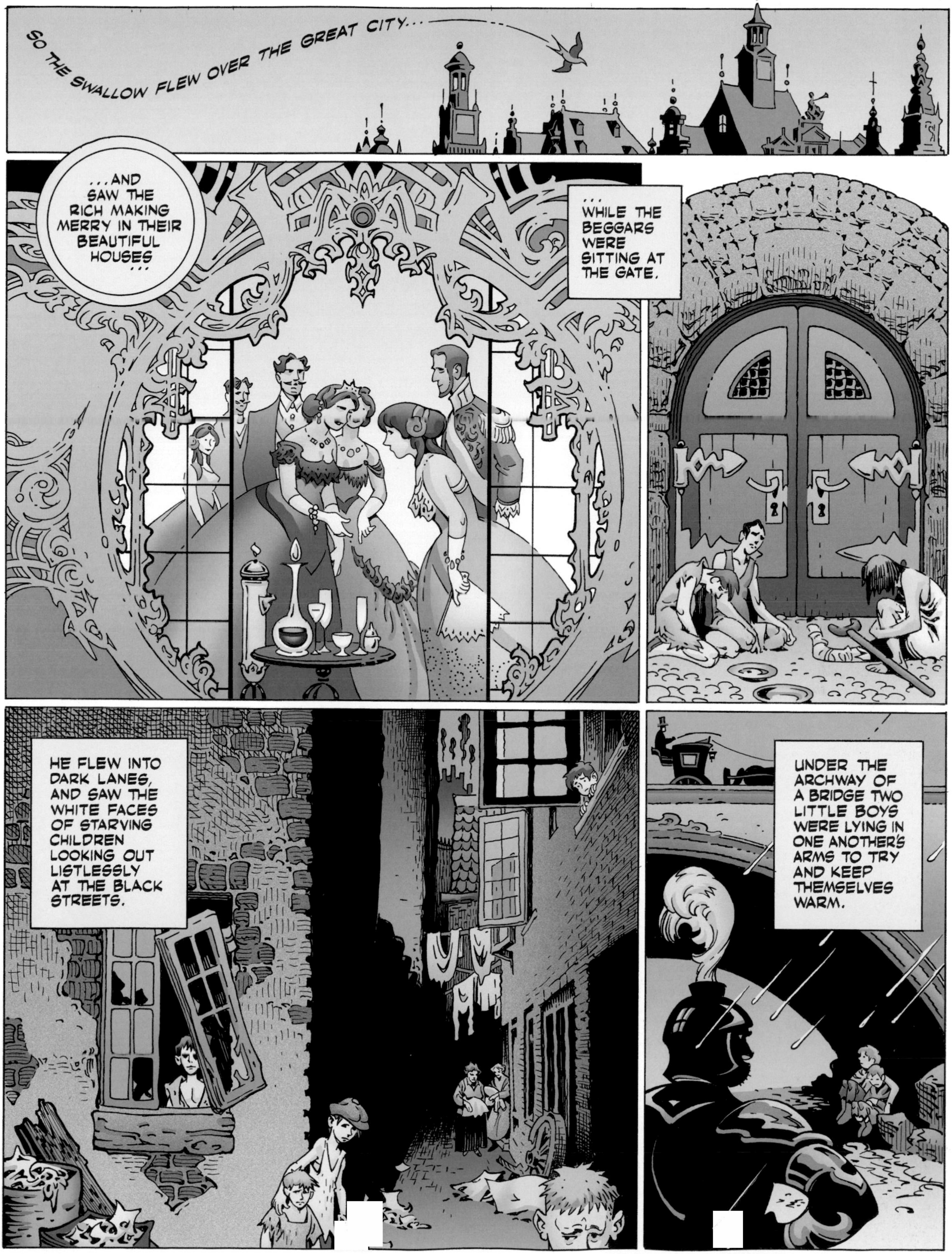
SO THE SWALLOW FLEW OVER THE GREAT CITY...
...AND SAW THE RICH MAKING MERRY IN THEIR BEAUTIFUL HOUSES ...
... WHILE THE BEGGARS WERE SITTING AT THE GATE.
HE FLEW INTO DARK LANES, AND SAW THE WHITE FACES OF STARVING CHILDREN LOOKING OUT LISTLESSLY AT THE BLACK STREETS.
UNDER THE ARCHWAY OF A BRIDGE TWO LITTLE BOYS WERE LYING IN ONE ANOTHER'S ARMS TO TRY AND KEEP THEMSELVES WARM.

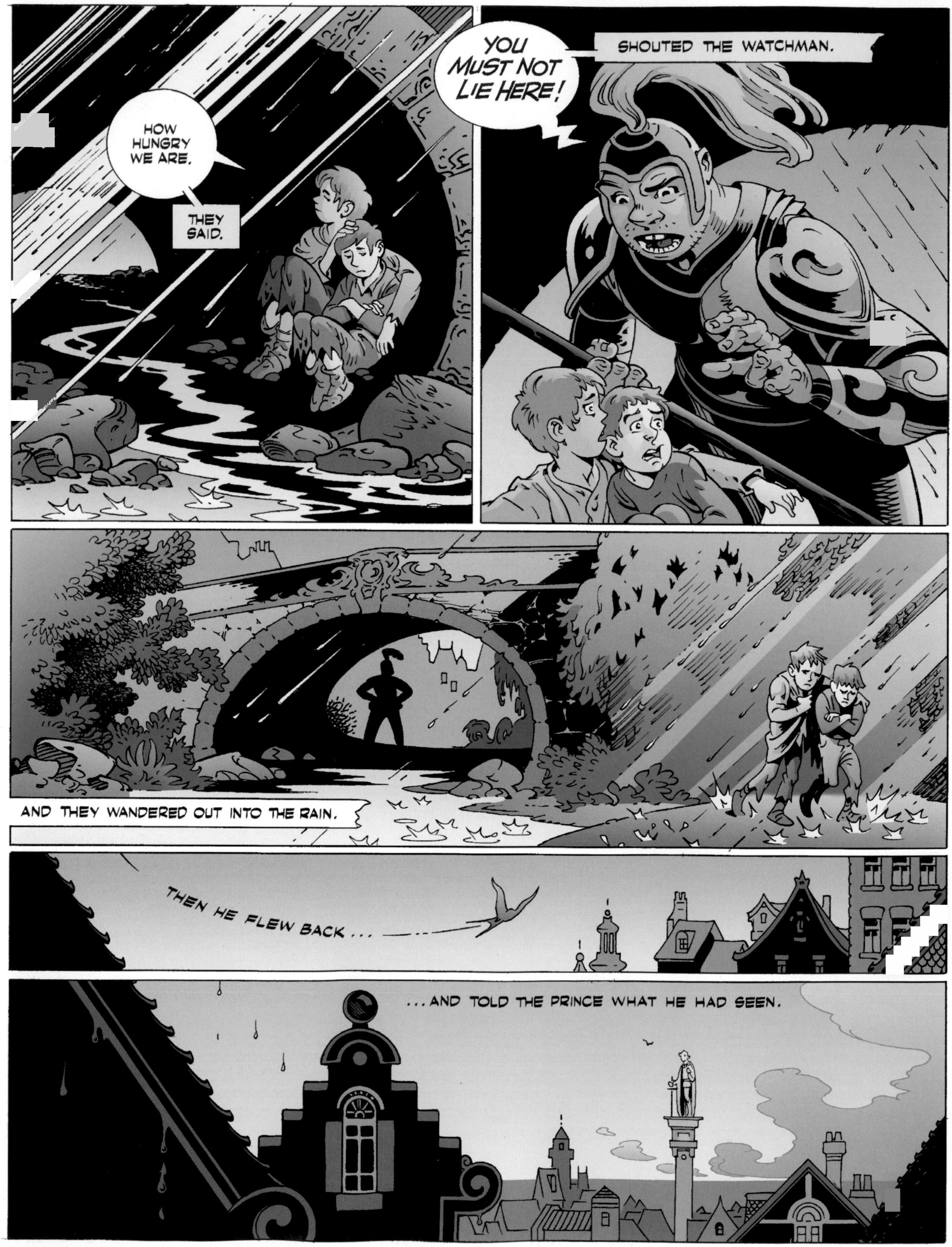
HOW HUNGRY WE ARE.
THEY SAID.
YOU MUST NOT LIE HERE!
SHOUTED THE WATCHMAN.
AND THEY WANDERED OUT INTO THE RAIN.
THEN HE FLEW BACK . . .
. . . AND TOLD THE PRINCE WHAT HE HAD SEEN.

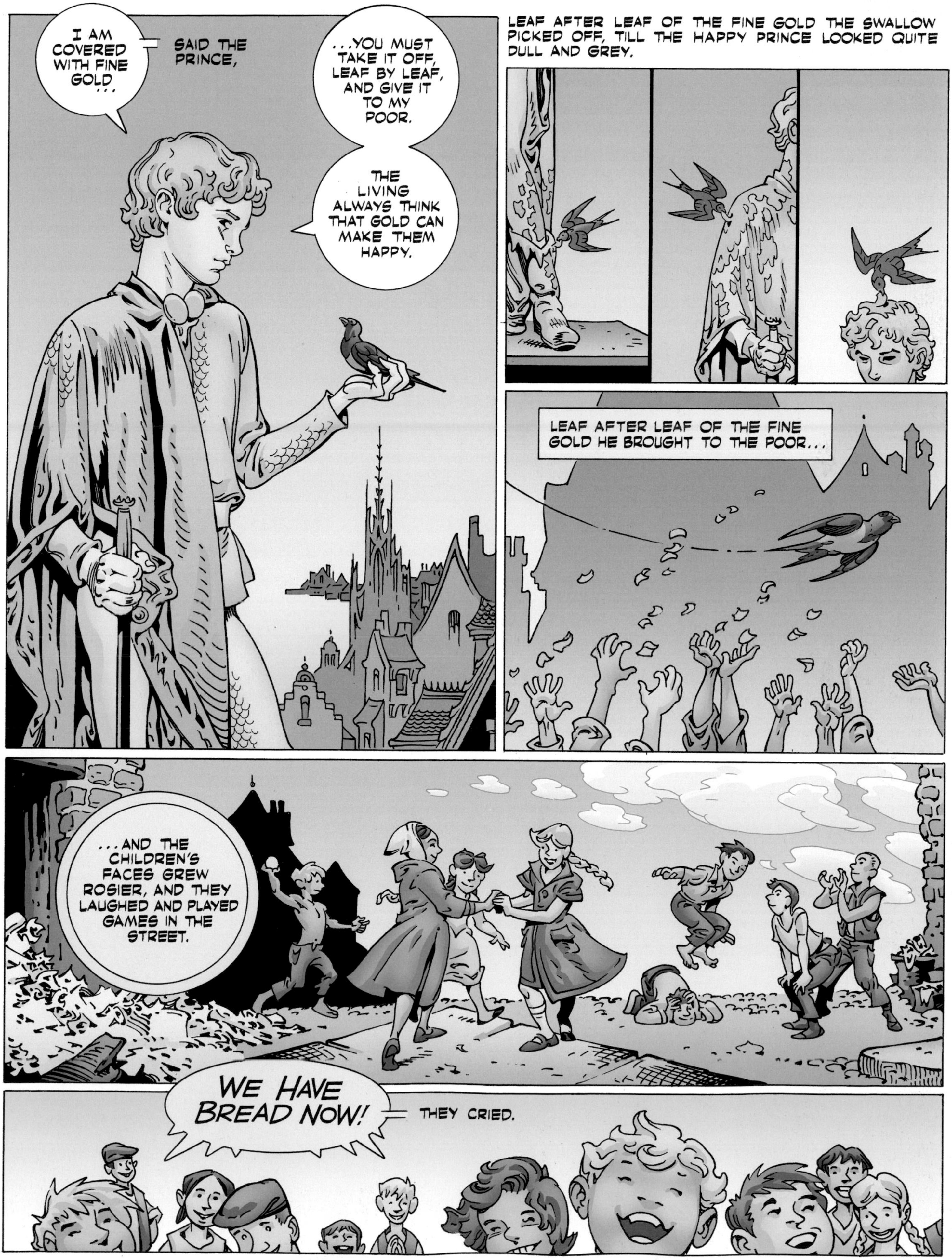
I AM COVERED WITH FINE GOLD...
SAID THE PRINCE,
...YOU MUST TAKE IT OFF, LEAF BY LEAF, AND GIVE IT TO MY POOR.
THE LIVING ALWAYS THINK THAT GOLD CAN MAKE THEM HAPPY.
LEAF AFTER LEAF OF THE FINE GOLD THE SWALLOW PICKED OFF, TILL THE HAPPY PRINCE LOOKED QUITE DULL AND GREY.
LEAF AFTER LEAF OF THE FINE GOLD HE BROUGHT TO THE POOR...
...AND THE CHILDREN'S FACES GREW ROSIER, AND THEY LAUGHED AND PLAYED GAMES IN THE STREET.
WE HAVE BREAD NOW!
THEY CRIED.

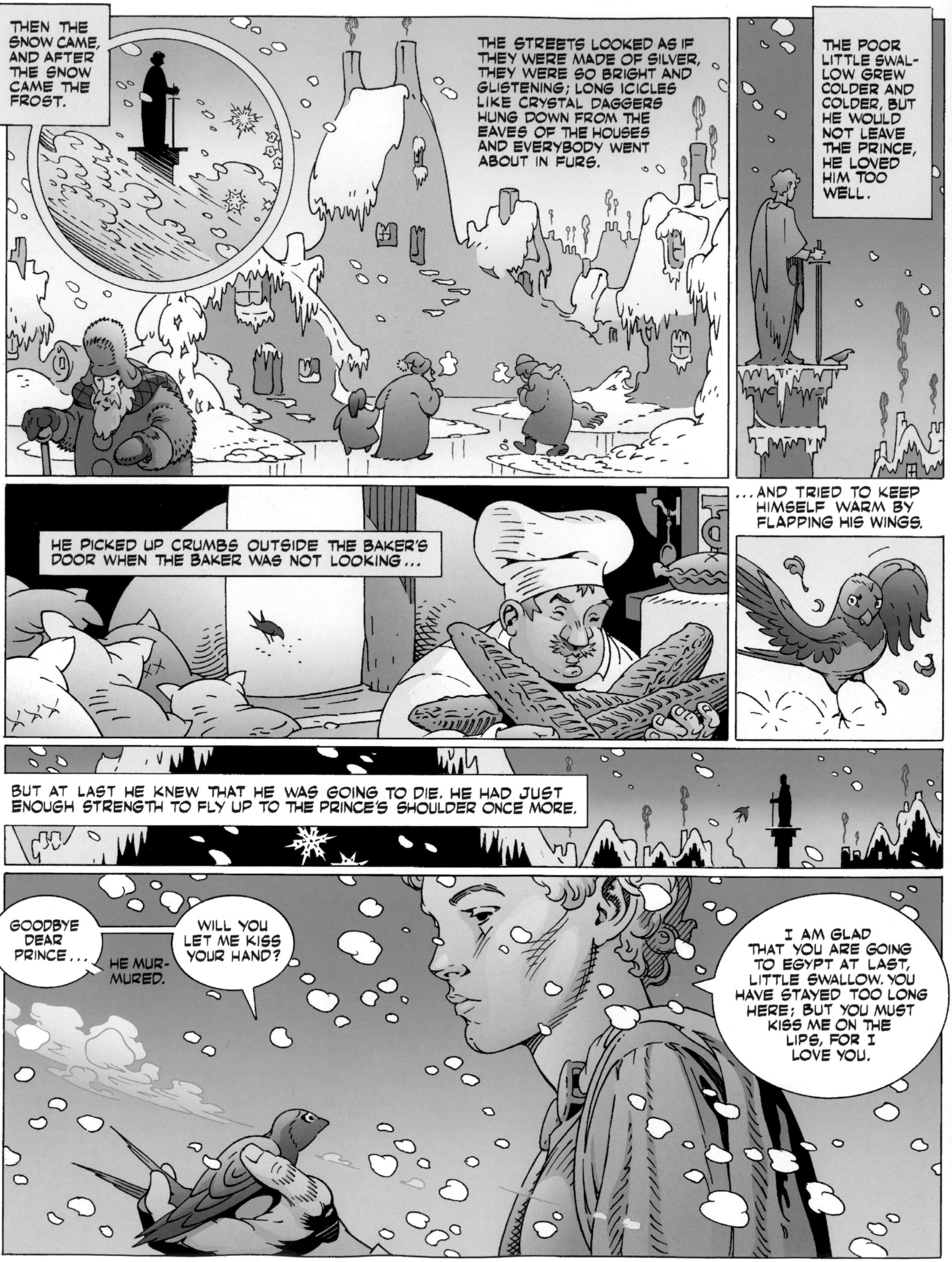
THEN THE SNOW CAME, AND AFTER THE SNOW CAME THE FROST.
THE STREETS LOOKED AS IF THEY WERE MADE OF SILVER, THEY WERE SO BRIGHT AND GLISTENING; LONG ICICLES LIKE CRYSTAL DAGGERS HUNG DOWN FROM THE EAVES OF THE HOUSES AND EVERYBODY WENT ABOUT IN FURS.
THE POOR LITTLE SWALLOW GREW COLDER AND COLDER, BUT HE WOULD NOT LEAVE THE PRINCE, HE LOVED HIM TOO WELL.
HE PICKED UP CRUMBS OUTSIDE THE BAKER'S DOOR WHEN THE BAKER WAS NOT LOOKING...
...AND TRIED TO KEEP HIMSELF WARM BY FLAPPING HIS WINGS.
BUT AT LAST HE KNEW THAT HE WAS GOING TO DIE. HE HAD JUST ENOUGH STRENGTH TO FLY UP TO THE PRINCE'S SHOULDER ONCE MORE.
GOODBYE DEAR PRINCE...
HE MURMURED.
WILL YOU LET ME KISS YOUR HAND?
I AM GLAD THAT YOU ARE GOING TO EGYPT AT LAST, LITTLE SWALLOW. YOU HAVE STAYED TOO LONG HERE; BUT YOU MUST KISS ME ON THE LIPS, FOR I LOVE YOU.

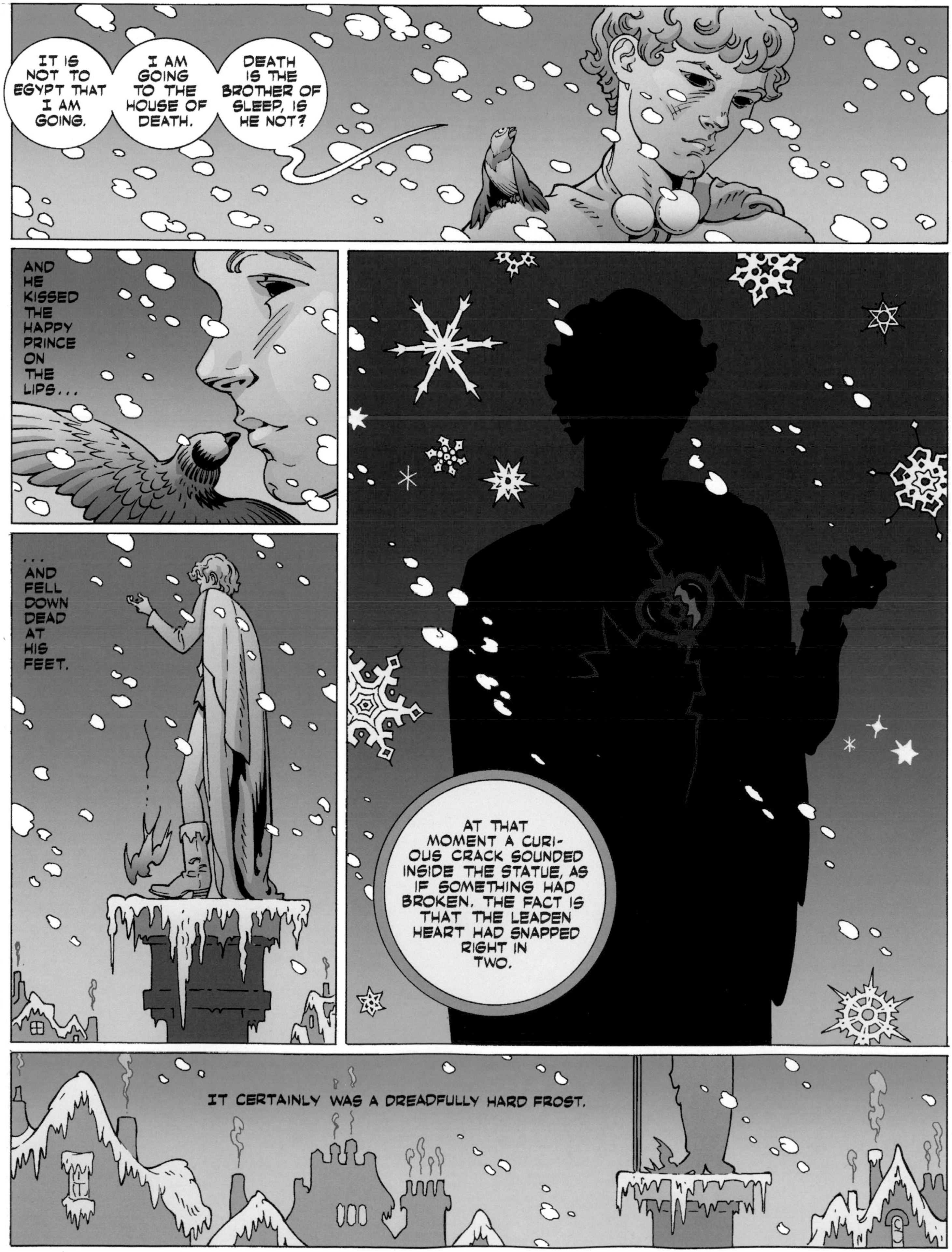
IT IS NOT TO EGYPT THAT I AM GOING.
I AM GOING TO THE HOUSE OF DEATH.
DEATH IS THE BROTHER OF SLEEP, IS HE NOT?
AND HE KISSED THE HAPPY PRINCE ON THE LIPS...
... AND FELL DOWN DEAD AT HIS FEET.
AT THAT MOMENT A CURIOUS CRACK SOUNDED INSIDE THE STATUE, AS IF SOMETHING HAD BROKEN. THE FACT IS THAT THE LEADEN HEART HAD SNAPPED RIGHT IN TWO.
IT CERTAINLY WAS A DREADFULLY HARD FROST.

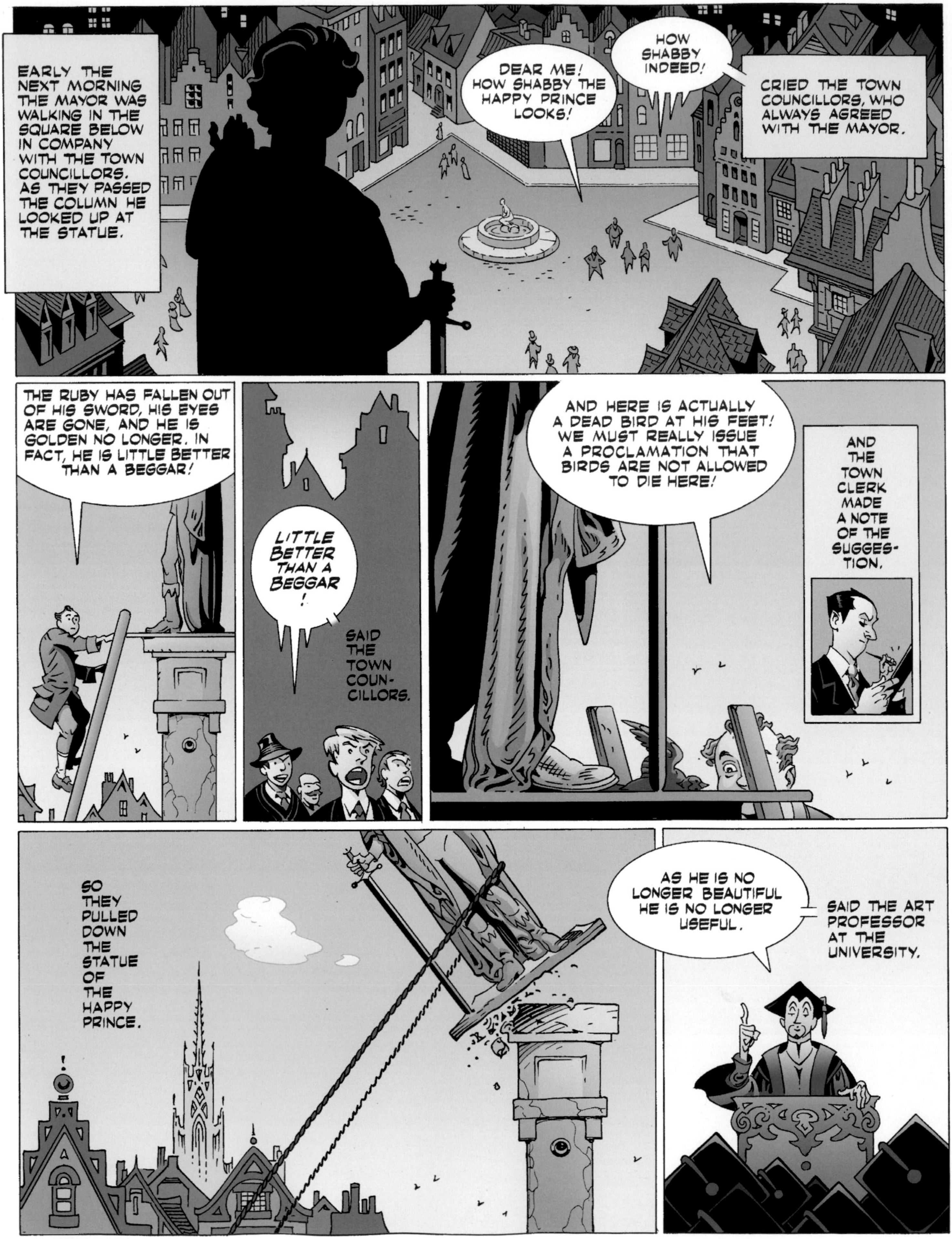
EARLY THE NEXT MORNING THE MAYOR WAS WALKING IN THE SQUARE BELOW IN COMPANY WITH THE TOWN COUNCILLORS. AS THEY PASSED THE COLUMN HE LOOKED UP AT THE STATUE.
DEAR ME! HOW SHABBY THE HAPPY PRINCE LOOKS!
HOW SHABBY INDEED!
CRIED THE TOWN COUNCILLORS, WHO ALWAYS AGREED WITH THE MAYOR.
THE RUBY HAS FALLEN OUT OF HIS SWORD, HIS EYES ARE GONE, AND HE IS GOLDEN NO LONGER. IN FACT, HE IS LITTLE BETTER THAN A BEGGAR!
LITTLE BETTER THAN A BEGGAR!
SAID THE TOWN COUNCILLORS.
AND HERE IS ACTUALLY A DEAD BIRD AT HIS FEET! WE MUST REALLY ISSUE A PROCLAMATION THAT BIRDS ARE NOT ALLOWED TO DIE HERE!
AND THE TOWN CLERK MADE A NOTE OF THE SUGGESTION.
SO THEY PULLED DOWN THE STATUE OF THE HAPPY PRINCE.
AS HE IS NO LONGER BEAUTIFUL HE IS NO LONGER USEFUL.
SAID THE ART PROFESSOR AT THE UNIVERSITY.

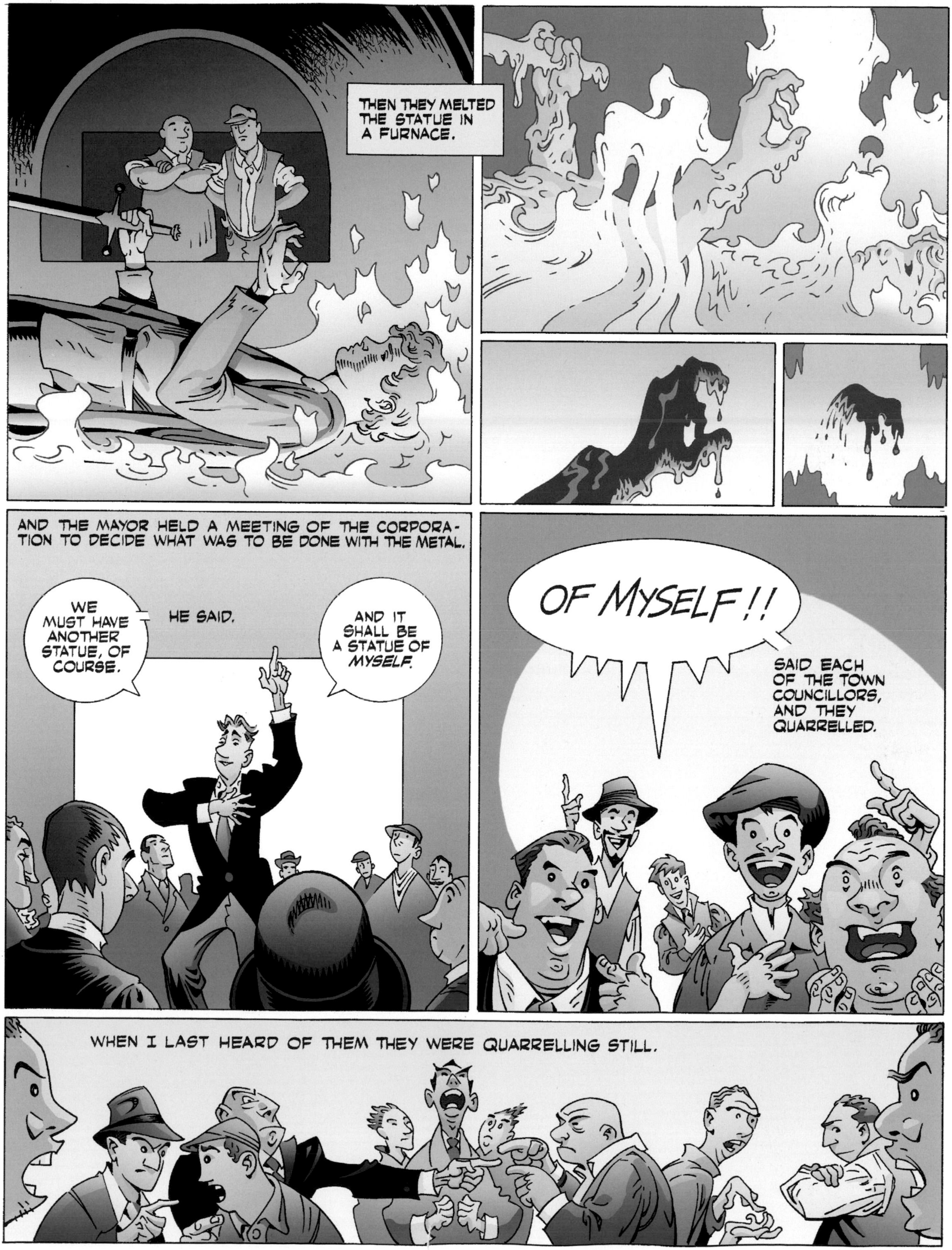
THEN THEY MELTED THE STATUE IN A FURNACE.
AND THE MAYOR HELD A MEETING OF THE CORPORATION TO DECIDE WHAT WAS TO BE DONE WITH THE METAL.
WE MUST HAVE ANOTHER STATUE, OF COURSE.
HE SAID.
AND IT SHALL BE A STATUE OF *MYSELF*.
OF MYSELF!!
SAID EACH OF THE TOWN COUNCILLORS, AND THEY QUARRELLED.
WHEN I LAST HEARD OF THEM THEY WERE QUARRELLING STILL.

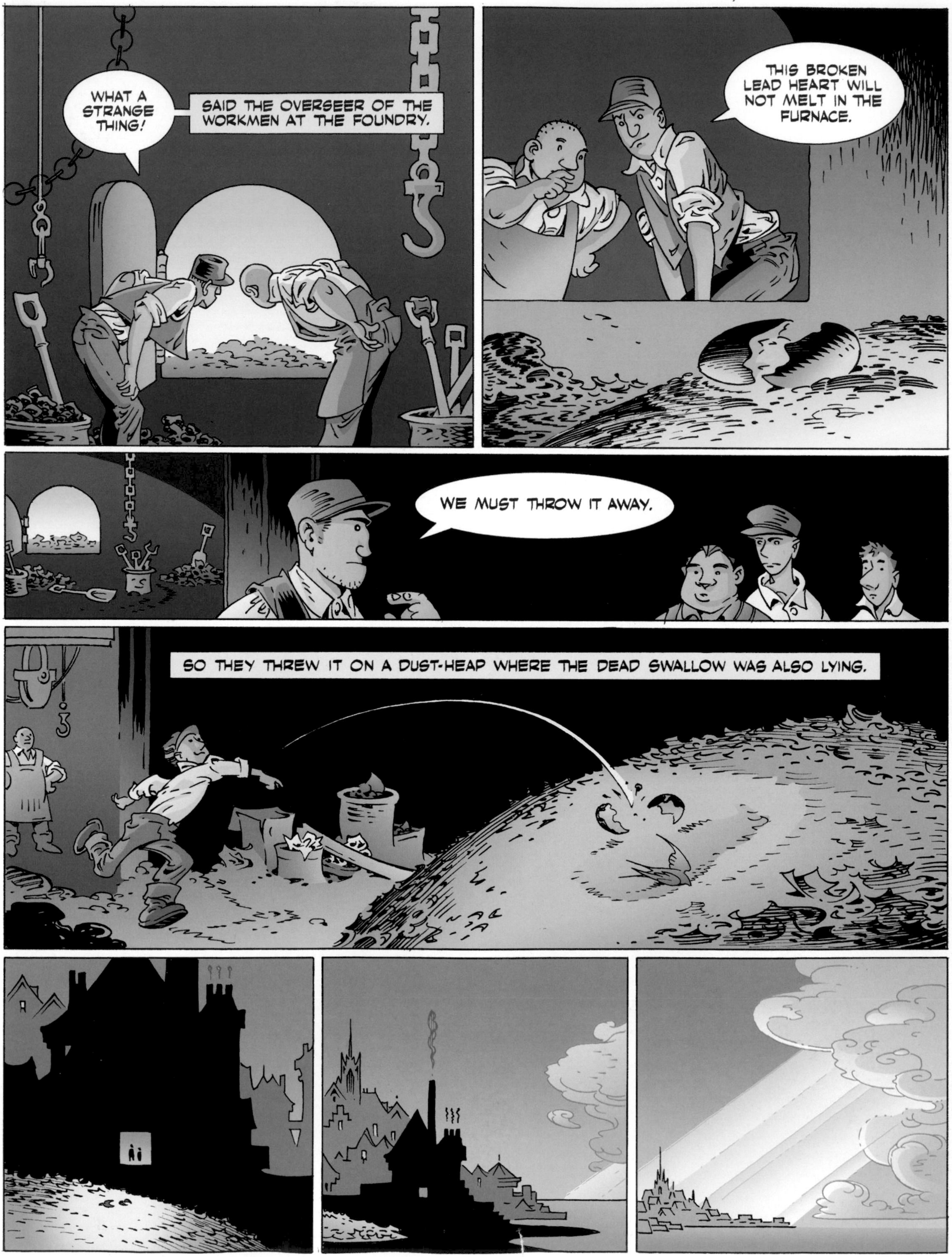
WHAT A STRANGE THING!
SAID THE OVERSEER OF THE WORKMEN AT THE FOUNDRY.
THIS BROKEN LEAD HEART WILL NOT MELT IN THE FURNACE.
WE MUST THROW IT AWAY.
SO THEY THREW IT ON A DUST-HEAP WHERE THE DEAD SWALLOW WAS ALSO LYING.

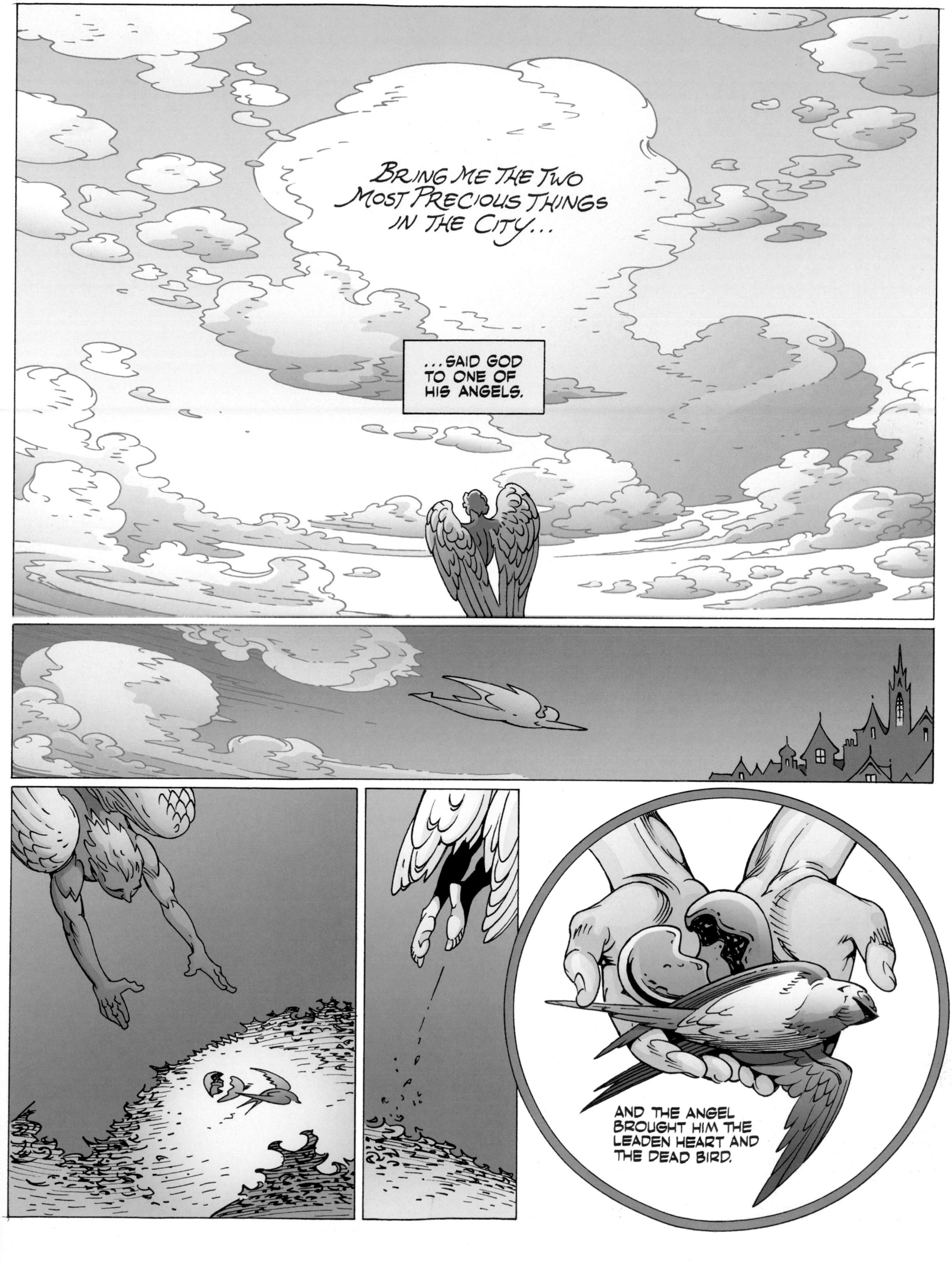
BRING ME THE TWO MOST PRECIOUS THINGS IN THE CITY...
...SAID GOD TO ONE OF HIS ANGELS.
AND THE ANGEL BROUGHT HIM THE LEADEN HEART AND THE DEAD BIRD.

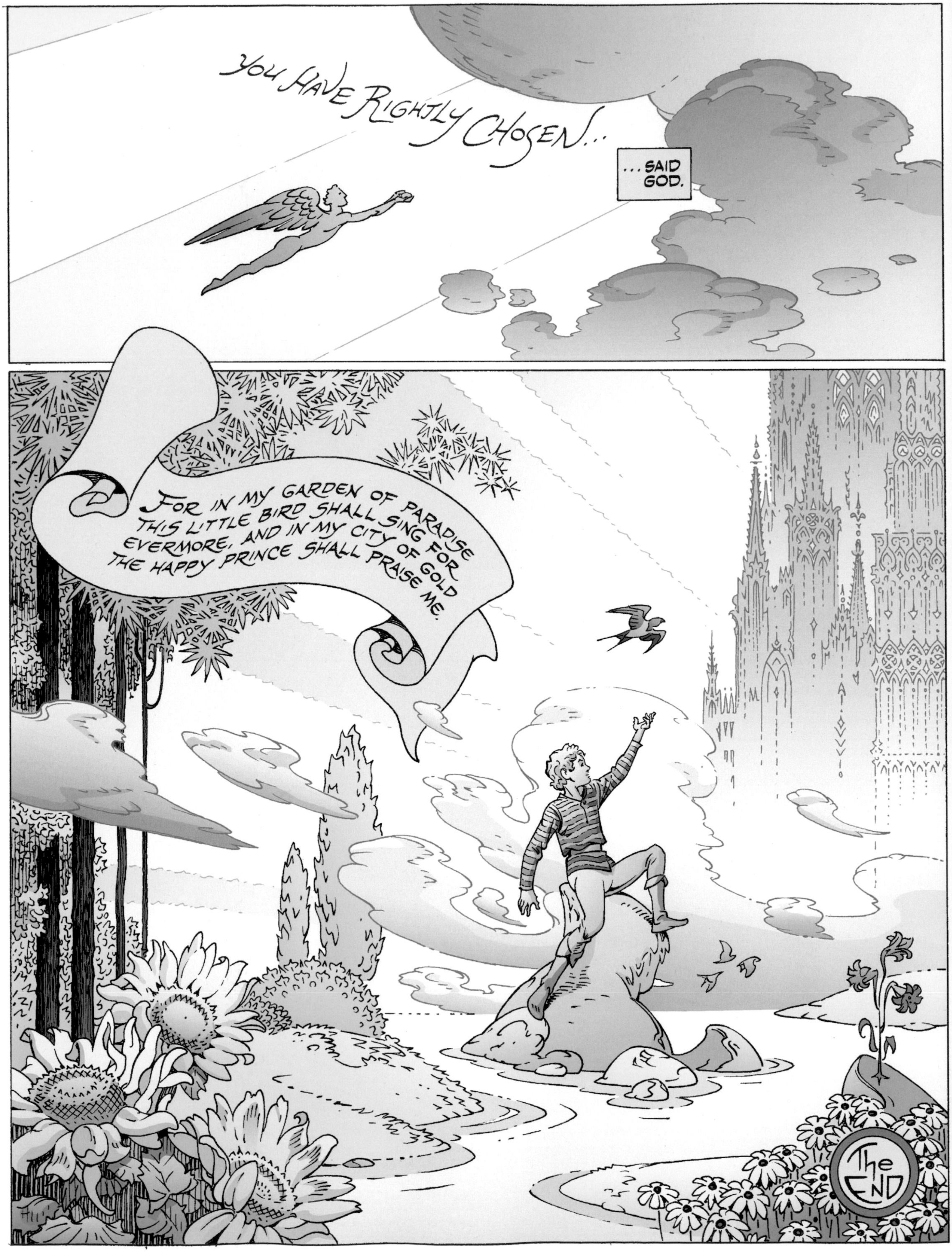

YOU HAVE RIGHTLY CHOSEN...
...SAID GOD.
FOR IN MY GARDEN OF PARADISE THIS LITTLE BIRD SHALL SING FOR EVERMORE, AND IN MY CITY OF GOLD THE HAPPY PRINCE SHALL PRAISE ME.
THE END